TREASURES OF THE UNSEEN
UNDER THE SOUL SERIES
BOOK ONE

JENNIFER OAKS

Original Manuscript Edited by
LIAM J CROSS
Cover Design by
SARAH

OAKFEATHER
PUBLISHING

Treasures of the Unseen
Copyright © 2018, 2026 by Jennifer Oaks
All rights reserved.

Published by **Oak Feather Publishing**

Treasures of the Unseen is the first book in the *Under the Soul* Series.

ISBN: 978-1-7753902-1-3 (paperback)
ISBN: 978-1-7753902-0-6 (ebook)

Cover Images Licensed from © Shutterstock
Cover Design by Sarah Smith
Original Manuscript Edited by Liam J Cross

DEDICATION

"Everything is temporary, emotions, thoughts, people and scenery. Do not become attached, just flow with it."

— Prince_ea

PROLOGUE

THE PINK TREE

"Daddy! Daddy! Mommy home!" Gabrielle shouted, relieved to hear the roaring of her mother's car coming in the driveway. She had spent the last few days looking out the window, wondering when her mother would be back.

Without hesitation, she ran to the front door. Her little toes lifted her body, and her ginger curls bounced to the feel of her excitement. She grabbed the doorknob, twisted it, and ran outside.

"Wait... Wait for me..." her father said, running behind her.

Gabrielle barely gave her mother a moment to set down her bags before rushing over and squeezing her leg. Each tiny toe-lift brought her closer, her bangs bouncing with every step.

"Oh, my beautiful Pumpkin! Come here and give Mommy a hug. Hmm... you smell like strawberry shortcake. Did you have your bath?"

"Mmm-hmm."

1

"And your new dress too!"

"Mmm-hmm."

Her mother tilted her head. "You did."

Though her dress was half tucked into her leggings, she twirled as if she had spent half a day getting ready for the most important rehearsal of her life.

"For dance! Member? You said!"

"Of course I remember. How could I forget?"

John moved closer, his arm encircling his wife's waist before leaning in to kiss her. "Welcome home, sweet ballerina. Let me give you a hand." He grabbed the luggage and carried it inside.

"Mommy!" Gabrielle tugged at her mother's dress—five, six times. "Mommy, pleeeease! Dance!"

"You want to see my new moves?" Charlotte climbed the front set of stairs and walked through the unfinished entry. "We learned so much in such a short time my head still spins."

Gabrielle's brow furrowed at the unfamiliar word. "Ssspppiiin?"

They stepped into the living room, where the notes of classical music mingled with the scent of freshly cut flowers.

"Kin kin!" Gabrielle shouted, her hands up in the air, ready for the swirls. At three years old, she couldn't quite say her full nickname correctly, and her squeaky version always made her mother smile.

"Yes," Charlotte said, eyes following her daughter's arms. "Spin, spin, my little Kin Kin."

And they danced for what seemed like hours, their rhythm only broken by the ringing phone.

John walked into the kitchen, eyes fixed on his wife and daughter, and brought the receiver to his ear.

"Hello, John speaking."

"Hi, Mr. Arseneault. It's Dr. Scott. May I speak to your wife?"

"Is something wrong?"

"I'm afraid I cannot speak to you—patient confidentiality."

"Oh, okay. I understand. Just a second."

John set the phone down and walked into the living room. The sun was setting, casting strong reddish hues across the room. "Honey, there's someone on the line for you."

"Who is it?"

"Dr. Scott."

Charlotte's face went pale. Whiter than a winter night. She let go of Gabrielle's hands and clutched her stomach.

"Are you okay?" John asked.

Without answering, she walked into the kitchen and picked up the phone. Pressing a hand to her chest, she searched for a breath that refused to come.

"Hi, Charlotte, Dr. Scott. I'm afraid I have bad news. The results came back, and they aren't encouraging."

Charlotte looked at her husband, unable to speak. Her knees buckled, and she collapsed onto the unvarnished floor.

"Hello? Hello?" the doctor's voice echoed in the silence.

"It's me, Dr.," John mumbled.

"I will need to see your wife. Please have her come to my office first thing tomorrow morning."

"I'll pass on the message."

The line went silent.

John knelt beside Charlotte, wordless, wrapping his arms around her. He ran his hand through her hair and welcomed the tears.

Gabrielle walked up slowly, hands behind her back. "Why Mommy sad?"

John pulled their daughter close and held her tight. "It will be alright, Pumpkin... it will be alright."

"SHE IS SO YOUNG... I have fought with all my heart John, but... but I can't anymore. I will miss her terribly. Such a beautiful life I will miss," Charlotte said, with water in her eyes. "I'm so sorry. There is nothing else I can do but breathe and let go. But why is this happening? I don't know. It is impossible to understand such fate. She doesn't deserve to grow up without a mother by her side. Maybe I should've taken the medication..."

"Shh... Don't torture yourself. You did what was best. I am proud of you."

"I thought I could fight this thing on my own."

"And you did. Honey, you were brave and fought this with all your heart. You handled it with such grace. For you, and for her. And don't forget... You will be dearly missed, but your spirit will remain with us, always."

"Thank you. I love you so much."

John left a soft kiss on her forehead. "I love you too, darling."

As the moment drew closer, she allowed the inner peace to wash away her fear and regret. "Bring her to me," she whispered.

John stood up and called for Gabrielle. A few seconds later, she appeared in the doorway. Uneven wrinkles marred the hem of her polka-dot dress, one sleeve slipping off her shoulder. A smear of pink icing curved like a question mark across her belly, and the red ribbon her mother had gifted her slightly twisted.

4

"Yes, Mommy?"

"Come here," Charlotte said.

With John's help, Gabrielle climbed onto the bed next to her mother.

"Do you recall where you were before you had me as your mommy?"

"Yes," she replied.

"How was it?"

Gabrielle mingled her tiny fingers together, pressed her arms on the mattress, and gazed at the empty space between her and the ceiling. "Oh, it was beautiful. White. Sunny. Always happy."

"I think that is where Mommy is going."

"Me too?"

"No, not for now, Pumpkin. Not for now." She reached for Gabrielle's hands. "You still have games to play and so much love to give. One day, you'll be all grown up and you'll amaze the world. But remember—I'll always be with you. I'll remain forever seated by the light in your heart."

Tears welled up in Gabrielle's eyes, each hesitant to meet her cheeks.

"But Mommy, you promised we'd dance tomorrow."

"If you close your eyes, I'll be right there, and we'll dance till the sun goes down."

"Until I fall asleep?"

"Until you fall asleep, my love."

"You promise?"

"I promise."

The little girl leaned in for one last hug. "I love you, Mommy."

"I love you too, Pumpkin."

After releasing the embrace, Gabrielle wiped the tears from

her mother's face and whispered into her ear, "When you get there, find the pink tree, okay? I was never alone there."

Charlotte smiled through her tears, brushing Gabrielle's curls one last time. "I know, sweetheart. I know. You were never alone."

1

13 YEARS

"Gabrielle! Your taxi's here. Do you need help?" John asked at the bottom of the old maple staircase.

Gabrielle shouted from her bedroom. "No Daddy, I'm fine. Give me a moment, I'm coming down."

Even if thirteen years had passed, the memory of her last moment with her mother was as clear as spring water. She looked at her reflection in the mirror above her desk and wiped a tear from her face.

"We'll dance till the sun goes down," she heard. The voice was soft, familiar, comforting—like the taste of freshly baked bread, still warm from the oven, topped with a pat of sweet, melting butter.

Behind her reflection stood Charlotte—young and beautiful, just as she was back then.

"Mom? I miss you so much," Gabrielle said. She wanted to turn around and hold her one more time, but knew too well the vision wasn't real.

Charlotte raised her arm, her fingertips brushing Gabrielle's shoulder. "All will be fine, Kin Kin. I know it wasn't easy growing up without a mother. I'm sorry. You've had your share of darkness, but I'm afraid we can't go without it. I came to tell you something before you leave. You are strong—but don't forget to listen to your heart. It will guide you far better than anything else."

Charlotte's ghost faded.

"Mommy, wait... I... I don't feel the light in my heart anymore. What happened? How can I find it again?"

"Follow the signs. Pay close attention," Charlotte said, just before her reflection disappeared.

"No... don't leave." Gabrielle lowered her head, covering her eyes with trembling hands. "I need you..."

With emotions pressing from every angle, Gabrielle took a few seconds to retouch her makeup. She didn't want her smeared eyes to raise questions—the transition was already heavy enough for her and her father. She retrieved the red ribbon from the top drawer, the faint scent of sandalwood clinging to it, and bound her hair in a high ponytail.

She walked to the other side of the bed and gazed out at the playground where she had spent her childhood, its rusty swings swaying violently in the wind. Dark clouds pushed north, promising a massive storm. The echoes of laughter, scraped knees, and small victories seemed to rise from the earth itself, carrying both warmth and longing. Each memory, more vivid than the last, was carefully preserved, like autumn leaves pressed between the pages of a book.

Before Gabrielle was born, John and Charlotte had made an offer on this two-story cottage, its white picket fence already weathered by time. Since the owner had passed, the bank was only interested in the minimum payment to close the loan. The deal was too good to refuse.

Imperfect as it was, the house thrummed with the promise

of renewed life—laughter and dreams waiting to be made real within its walls. John had dreamed of renovating it, pouring his hope and plans into what could be, while Charlotte pursued her ambitions as a professional ballet dancer. But as time went on, and his hair grew greyer, his dream never came to pass.

Suitcase in hand, Gabrielle walked down the stairs to where her father waited. To her surprise, he looked much older than he actually was.

"Your ride is waiting outside," her father said. "I told him you'd be there in a few minutes. I must say I'm glad our neighbor agreed to take you to the airport. You know it's been forever since I drove out of town."

Gabrielle noticed his hands tucked deep within the worn, rough pockets of his trousers.

"It's alright, Daddy. Everything's gonna be fine." She knew him well enough to catch the hint of concern in his eyes.

After the death of his wife, John had somehow felt inadequate to take on the emotional challenge of raising a little girl on his own. He had been genuinely competent in the more stereotypical male role and had seen great success in providing a roof, food, clothes and a helping hand for school, but when it came down to the harsh internal logistics of understanding the emotional waves of a human being, he more often than not bailed from it.

"Do you have everything you need?" John said, swirling his foot on the hardwood floor, mimicking the movement of his thoughts. His eyes, restless too, never came up to meet Gabrielle's.

"Don't worry, Daddy," Gabrielle said. Her hand moved toward his arm, then fell back to her side. "If I need anything, I have someone I can ask. Nadia is a great friend."

"Good. I guess I'll be seeing you next summer, then," he said, reaching for Gabrielle's suitcase.

"I'll stay for a couple of months. This will give us some time to catch up." With a playful whiff, she smiled from the corner of her eye. "Take care of yourself, Daddy... and don't do anything stupid."

"If by 'stupid' you mean doing anything at all, don't worry —I'm way above that."

The sound of their forced laughter echoed through the hall.

"Daddy?"

"Yes, Pumpkin?"

"Thank you for everything you've done. You've been a remarkable father—and one hell of a mother. I know today isn't easy. I have my share of uncomfortable feelings too, and I don't quite know what to do with them. But I know you both loved me more than I'll ever be able to love myself. Thank you for that." She jumped into his unready arms. "I love you so much, Daddy."

He clung to the suitcase in one arm and Gabrielle in the other.

"I love you too."

A strong wind made its way into the house, pushing through the front door and taking down the coat rack. The sound of the metal slamming the wooden floor caught them off guard. It was not unusual for this part of the land, but somehow this one felt different. The screen door bounced against the wall, making John smile.

"Must be your mother coming to wish you good luck. I remember how she used to rush into the house when she had something exciting to say, leaving the door wide open. This sound used to drive me crazy. It's funny how it's those little things you miss the most."

"Are you gonna be okay, Daddy?"

"Yeah, I'll be fine. You know, I've never been too good with all this," John said, his hand gesturing at the space in front of his chest. "Now that you're going, I'm suddenly thinking about my life. This house was my dream. Your mother wandered around the world, and that was fine with me. Watching her shine made me happy. What I realize now is that I embraced her dream but left mine on the shelf. Even after she left, I still felt too guilty to do anything about it. But today it's different. Today, I want to."

"That's great! Know that you have both our permissions to do as you please with the house," Gabrielle said.

He raised his eyebrows. "I never thought I needed permission for that, but thanks. It feels good. So… at what time is your flight?"

"One-forty-five. I'll land at around eight-forty. I'll text you before bed."

"Yeah, that would be nice. You know, your old father is still worried about his little girl."

John walked out of the house, stood on the porch, and filled his lungs with a deep breath. Gabrielle followed.

After greeting their neighbor, John opened the backseat door. Gabrielle climbed in, and he placed her suitcase beside her, closing the door gently before leaning on the open window.

"Have a safe trip."

"Thanks, Daddy."

As the car drove away, she watched the house—and her father—disappear into the distance. She leaned back against the worn leather seat, letting the hum of the road carry her forward.

2

THIRTY THOUSAND FEET

*G*abrielle stepped out of the car, a rush of euphoria flooding her body. It was 1 p.m., yet the horizon had dimmed into an eerie green, hovering with strange intention. Heavy clouds pressed low, swallowing the distance. Even the wind seemed to join the moment, its sharp gusts tugging at loose objects, rattling doors, stirring up anxieties.

With a thank you to their neighbour, Gabrielle left the car and took in the scene. Her stress level went up like a child on their first day of swimming lessons.

Small planes waited patiently, a faint shimmer clinging to their wings, as if they knew the secret path to an unclaimed future.

Behind them stood the control tower, bold in deep blue, squinting at the horizon through its glassy eyes. It wasn't a fancy airport. Not even comfortable. In all honesty, it was quite forgettable, if not for the views. But to really see it all, you'd have to be flying, which Gabrielle had never done before.

Around her, the ground crew members moved in, heads

down, voices clipped as the first growl of thunder rolled in like a throat clearing in warning.

She held on to her ticket—her boarding pass folded tight in her hand. Montreal was only a quick hop away, but it might as well have been another universe. She glanced one last time over her shoulder at the stretch of land and sea she called home for just long enough to fall in love with it all over again.

She grabbed her bag and stepped through the front door, finding herself face to face with the only check-in counter in the building.

"One suitcase, Ma'am?"

"Yes. That will be all, thank you."

The agent glanced at the pass, tapped a few keys on his keyboard, and said something that sounded very much like: *"Yup, you're off to the big city, Ma'am."*

"Thank you," Gabrielle said, before turning away to face the waiting room.

She eyed the boarding screen, her flight coming into view. Forty-five minutes until takeoff.

"Now what?" she whispered, drifting toward the seating area. She sat down, tucked her bag behind her head, and closed her eyes.

"Pay attention," she heard. "Follow the signs," the voice continued.

Gabrielle opened her eyes.

The voice wasn't her mother's ghost this time.

Before her stood an old woman with long straight white hair, a purple trench coat, and black vintage rubber boots.

Startled, Gabrielle gripped the arms of her chair.

"Don't be afraid, my child. Don't be afraid."

Gabrielle glanced around, hoping no one had witnessed the scene.

…They had.

And judging by their baffled looks, they seemed grateful the strange old woman had chosen a different target for her cosmic theatrics.

Inside the hoody of her raincoat, the old woman's face somehow seemed smooth and incredibly soft. Gabrielle thought she looked like a modern witch who had traded her superpowers for longevity. But even from her certain age, she hadn't lost her inner child's spirit. She was wearing deep plum lipstick and smoky eyeshadow. And more impressively, looked good doing so.

The old woman leaned closer and whispered, "What's your name?"

"Gabrielle."

"Oh, sweet child. This is a remarkable name. I bet your mother loved you very much to give you such a name."

"Yes, she did," Gabrielle said, still looking around.

The old lady sat next to her, her coat dangling onto Gabrielle's chair. To avoid the touch, Gabrielle held on with a full grip, sitting herself up and leaning slightly to her right.

"My name is Dorothy. I'm traveling to see my grandson. He just had heart surgery. The doctors didn't know if he was going to make it, but he did. I'm so proud of him. Unlike me, he has his whole life in front of him. Well, here I am rambling about my story. But what about you, young lady? Where's the wind taking you today?"

"I'm going away to study dancing."

"Oh, that is lovely," the old lady said. "Ballet?"

"No. My mother studied ballet, but I wanted to try contemporary dance."

"That must be something. How about I take out my cards and do a little reading for you before you go?"

"That won't be necessary, thank you," Gabrielle said.

"Oh, it's on me. It's been so long since I did a reading. I always carry a deck with me just in case," Dorothy said, looking into her bag. Her eyes lit up. "Ah, there you are."

The cards had sparked the old lady's passion, and Gabrielle didn't want to ruin the moment. "Why not?" she finally said.

"Just close your eyes and think about a question or concern you might have. Something you would like more clarity on."

"Okay. Got it."

Dorothy mixed the cards and dropped the deck on her left thigh. With her right hand, she turned the first card from the deck. The Tower. "Oh my goodness," she said.

"What?" Gabrielle asked, moving to the edge of her seat, her eyes wanting more.

"You, my lady, are in for a little surprise. This card means that you are going to experience some radical changes through unexpected upheaval. Your world might fall apart, and you might feel confused, but go through it knowing something good is waiting for you on the other side. Just dance with the storm. One day soon, you'll look back and be glad it happened."

"What's the change? When will it happen?"

"My dear, no one can say, not even the cards. The Tower only suggests a sudden, unexpected incident that will change the course of your life. For a moment, you won't be able to tell which way is up and which way is down. What you must remember is that whatever happens, you are in the heart of it, experiencing the good and the bad. Don't forget, everything works together to bring you closer to your—"

A voice resonated through the main speaker, stopping

Dorothy's reading. "All passengers on the flight to Montreal should proceed to gate five for boarding."

"Well, I guess this is me," Gabrielle said as she stood.

"Enjoy your flight little one, and good luck with everything," the old lady said with a full smile.

"It was nice meeting you. Pass my best wishes on to your grandson."

"I will, my dear. I will."

Gabrielle followed the line to the plane, passed through the narrow hallway, and found her assigned seat. Beside the window, she sat down, lost in her thoughts about the old woman's story.

"A sudden change? A radical shift? Of course—I'm moving to a new city." With a roll of her eyes, she smirked at her own gullibility. "I can't believe I almost fell for it."

As passengers gained their seats, Gabrielle turned her gaze outside and stared at the ominous clouds. The thought of seeing the entire world through this tiny window suffocated her. She took a deep breath and closed her eyes. Whatever Dorothy's card had predicted, she wasn't ready to watch it unfold from 30,000 feet.

3

SAFE LANDING

The plane landed on time, and with the quick wash of relief came a revelation: the skies might have been her mother's joy, but they would never be hers. She much preferred the smooth, comforting rhythm of ground transportation. Less safe in theory, perhaps, but the wheels against the earth offered her the illusion of safety she needed.

When the plane screeched to a halt, she quickly stood, the smell of jet fuel thick in the air. She edged politely through the line of passengers, eager to step off at the first chance.

Once outside, she gave Nadia a call.

"Hey, it's me! Just landed."

"Awesome. The chauffeur should be there. Do you see him?"

Gabrielle looked around.

"Yup, I see him. Did he come up with the idea of the pink sparkling cardboard with my name on it?"

She laughed. "No, that was my idea. What, you don't like it?"

"It's perfect."

"I knew you'd like it. See ya in a bit!"

The chauffeur opened the door and carried Gabrielle's luggage to the back of the car.

Thirty minutes later, they arrived at Nadia's apartment.

Nadia's family owned the entire block—old houses squeezed tight against one another, their big windows framed by reddish-brown brick walls. One by one, they were being restored, and Nadia's was the first to shine with new life.

The chauffeur left the lights flashing, stepped out, and opened the door. Luggage in hand, he followed Gabrielle. They walked up the stairs to the second level. She pressed the doorbell—the brass cool beneath her fingertip—and a sharp electronic ping cut through the silence.

As soon as Nadia's dog heard the ring, he came rushing to the door, barking with excitement.

Nadia opened.

"Oh, Gaby, it's so nice to see you!"

The chauffeur dropped the suitcase by the door and walked out. He got in his car and drove away, leaving Gabrielle slightly confused.

"Don't worry about him—he doesn't talk much. Unlike this furry ball! His name's Mozart, by the way. The dog, I mean! And I think he already likes you."

Gabrielle knelt to pet him, savoring the warmth of his fur beneath her fingers.

"So, how was your trip? You must be exhausted," Nadia said.

"I'm okay, thanks. But I think I could definitely use a shower."

"Of course. Let me show you around, and then I'll leave you to it."

Gabrielle followed her as she weaved around Mozart's rubber toys scattered on the floor.

"This is the living room. Or if you prefer, Mozart's playground," she said, patting the top of his head. "Yes, Mommy's talking about you. You're a good boy. Oh yes, you are."

Gabrielle looked toward the living room windows. Squeezed between the curtains was an old wooden bench, topped with colorful throw pillows. She liked the one that read: *You are gorgeous* in shinny sparkles. She moved closer to take in the view—broad trees created shade and offered enough privacy for comfortable daydreaming sessions. A feature she knew she'd be using a lot.

They walked to the other side of the apartment, where the bedrooms were kept separate from the open-space layout.

"And here's your room. What do you think?"

The bedroom was on the small side, with a tall narrow window overlooking a red brick wall from the other building. She immediately noticed Nadia's vibrant decoration style. Crisp white walls flashing against the congo pink top duvet, an orangish tone of what seemed to be Nadia's favorite color: pink. The closet doors had been removed to provide more space, and on the right side of the bed, a three-drawer cabinet doubled as a nightstand and a dresser. Hand-painted black, with shiny gold knobs, it gave the room a bohemian feel.

"I like it a lot," Gabrielle replied.

"Alright, the bathroom is just in front, right there. Your towel's hanging behind the door. Let me know if you need anything."

"You're a lifesaver."

"Thank me later. Did you know my parents placed a bet on how long I could keep a roommate?" Nadia said with a wink, holding up her dog like a newborn baby. "I'll be in the kitchen if you need anything."

Gabrielle put her suitcase on the bed, took out her phone charger, and plugged in her phone.

Hey Daddy. I made it! Good night. xx

She pressed send and walked to the bathroom for a quick shower and new clothes. When she got out, she found Nadia in the kitchen crafting an evening snack. Mozart was sitting on one of the two bar stools, supervising the operation.

"Feeling better?"

"Oh yes. Much better. Hmm... it smells amazing! What is it?"

"Hope you're hungry."

"Starving!"

"I'm making my focaccia recipe. Well... it was actually my grandmother's, but I've added a few twists of my own. Let's eat before it cools," Nadia said, as Mozart's little tail wagged with excitement.

"Careful, Mozart—this one's for Gaby!"

"Wow, it's incredible. I've never tasted anything like this. You're becoming a hot mama, that's for sure."

"I know, right?" Nadia took a basket full of that delicious bread and walked to the living room. "So, are you ready for tomorrow?"

"How ready do I need to be?"

"You haven't heard?"

"Heard what?"

"We're going to be tested."

"Tested? What do you mean? We already went through weeks of auditions. Why would they do that?"

"To make sure we're all on the same page, I guess?"

"Well, in that case, no, I'm not ready." Gabrielle gave a nervous laugh. "Are you?"

"Are you crazy? I've been ready since the day I moved out of my parent's house. And believe me, I ain't going back."

"Well, I'd better get some rest if I don't want to be the first one back at the family home."

"But it's not even late."

"I'm solar-powered, remember?" Gabrielle yawned, quickly covering her mouth with her hand. "And it was a rough day."

"Alright then. Sweet dreams." Nadia picked up their plates and carried them to the kitchen. "Oh, before you go—I should mention I'm leaving early tomorrow. Erick's taking me out for breakfast before class, so we won't go together. Sorry."

"Sounds romantic. Don't worry about me; I'll be alright. We'll see each other in class."

"Have a good night."

"You too. And thanks for the snack."

Gabrielle walked to her room, and with barely enough energy to close the door behind her, she collapsed on the bed. The phone screen glowed from her nightstand, illuminating a single reply from her father—a heart. She tucked herself under the sheets and drifted off, forgetting to set her alarm.

RUNNING LATE

*G*abrielle woke up cuddled inside the sheets. Although the well-deserved comfort was tempting enough to spend the whole day there, she had somewhere else to be. She rubbed her eyes and reached for her phone. Ten-forty-five.

"Oh shit... I'm late."

She jumped out of bed, tied her hair into a messy ponytail, and threw on the first thing she could find: an oversized gray t-shirt with "Magic Numbers" printed on the back, and a pair of black leggings with mesh panels over the calves.

She walked out, her stomach rumbling, in search of a quick meal.

A small café caught her eye on the way to school. The smell of freshly baked pastries and simmering coffee wrapped around her as she stepped inside and joined the line.

She caught sight of the man in front of her, effortlessly stylish in a charcoal polo, dark navy trousers, and smoky glasses. His partially concealed tattoo, just peeking out from beneath his sleeve, grabbed her attention: a line of numbers. How clever.

The man turned around, lowered his glasses as if consciously opening a private space for both of them to enter. He allowed her to gaze into his eyes for a moment before shifting his attention down in front of her. "Isn't it a bit late for breakfast?" he said.

Gabrielle's cheeks turned red, matching the fiery hue of her hair. She looked down and forced a smile. "I overslept."

"That's okay. Never apologize for staying in bed."

He pulled his glasses up, paid for his meal and, with a polite "Bon appétit", gave Gabrielle a bow and left.

She stood still, mesmerized.

Those eyes. She'd never seen eyes this profoundly troubling. A sumptuous dark brown gaze, like rich chocolate melting under the tongue.

"That will be eleven twenty-three." The sound of the cash register's metallic clang snapped, bringing Gabrielle back to reality.

"Yes... yes, of course," she stammered, her fingers fumbling with the worn zipper of her bag before pulling out a twenty-dollar bill.

The doorbell chimed. Gabrielle glanced over her shoulder, catching a second look at the man. He held the door open for a group of young teenage girls—their giggles filling the space as they passed by. They whispered to one another words that could easily be imagined. He didn't even seem to notice; his eyes locked on hers.

With the flush of embarrassment rising to her face, she turned back and looked down again. The cashier handed her her change. She grabbed the five-dollar bill, but the coins slipped through her fingers. She left them scattered on the counter and quickly grabbed her meal. She walked to the exit, where she lingered a moment, her heart still racing as she watched his figure turn the corner and disappear.

She stepped outside and walked toward the school. His eyes lingered in her mind as she made her way through the bustling streets.

When she finally arrived in front of the building, she pulled a crumpled note from her bag.

It read: 1435 Bleury Street.

"Well, here we are," she said, looking up. The building stood there like a metronome between centuries—half modern, half keeper of secrets. Glass and graphite panels shimmered in the light, fracturing the street's reflections. The words ÉDIFICE WILDER - ESPACE DANSE stretched across its skin like a meaningful tattoo—sleek, unapologetic, almost daring you to look up and remember who you are.

To the left, brick bones of another era clung to the side like a memory that wouldn't fade. To the right, graffiti bloomed in rebellion, a burst of noise against the clean lines. Beneath her, the street pulsed with a steady heartbeat.

"Contemporary, it is," Gabrielle said, tossing her cardboard plate into the recycling bin. She rubbed her hands together, stepped forward, and pushed the front door.

"Can I help you, miss?" asked the concierge on duty.

"I'm looking for the dance school."

"It will be on your right. Take the elevator to the sixth floor."

"Thank you." Her words echoed in the cold, empty hall.

She made her way to the school's lobby, where a receptionist greeted her.

"May I have your name?"

"Gabrielle. Gabrielle Arsenault," she replied. "I'm sorry, I'm late."

"Here's today's agenda," the receptionist said. "The entrance to the studios is at the bottom of the stairs. Your group is now in Studio 5. I'll let them know you're here. Please be sure to close the door behind you."

Despite her racing heart and trembling hands, Gabrielle drew a deep breath, trying to still her mind and anchor herself in the present. Even with all her practice, she had only her gut to trust—a stubborn confidence insisting it would be alright. She inhaled once more, stepped downstairs, and opened the door.

With natural light pouring through the windows, the room felt bright, open, and airy—fresh out of the box. No scuff marks—just a gleaming floor and the trace of polish still lingering in the air. Under the curious gaze of her soon-to-be dance partners, Gabrielle scanned the room for a place to sit.

"Hello Gabrielle. Glad you found your way. Please take a seat. I believe that makes our group complete," the teacher said, ticking off her name on the blackboard behind him. "Like we were just discussing, we'll start today's training with a particular exercise. I want to see how you perform under pressure. Let me first show you the piece, and then we'll break it down into a sequence so you can make your way to the end. Music, please."

At the back of the room, a man sat at an old piano. After he pressed his fingers on the first few notes, the teacher began. His movements were precise yet tender, each gesture deliberate. His muscles, like well-tuned instruments, responded to each movement to perfection, leaving everyone amazed. Through the rise and fall of pliés, the tension of contractions, and the fluidity of steps, he crafted a memorable performance, both dynamic and unwavering.

When the music came to a full stop, he looked up at Gabrielle.

"Your turn," he said.

Taken by surprise, she stood and took her place in front of the group. Eyes closed, she struggled to remember the routine, but her mind raced through every detail—her body eager to release the tension that had built up over the past few days.

Once more, the man's fingers returned to the keys.

Gabrielle followed as if guided by an impulse to move and reach the intended expression of the initial piece.

"She has great flow," a student in the back whispered.

"And good at keeping the pace," another one said.

"That's pretty impressive, Gabrielle," the teacher said once the music stopped. "Now, let's start from the beginning. I want you to go further in this movement. You see, like this." He held her waist right to the limit of her lower curves. "Try to soften your head more. See how your body allows it. Keep your feet like this. It will be easier for you. Alright. Five, six, seven…"

The music filled the room again, and Gabrielle worked her magic one more time. Her moves flowed from instinct, each execution as smooth as the last. Her mother had taught her to memorize and internalize sequences long before she could speak full sentences. Where she had trouble, though, was in the movements themselves. She always felt she had to engage her whole body, her legs, her arms, even her toes, in everything she was doing. It had to be all or nothing.

"Good," he said, before addressing the group.

"If you are dancing in your living room for the sheer

27

pleasure of it, you don't need to worry about what I'm about to say. But if you're aiming for a professional career, conserving energy is key. Instead of engaging your whole body, like Gabrielle just did, focus on the critical muscles for each movement and allow the rest of your body to stay relaxed." He offered Gabrielle a thankful glance, inviting her back to her seat. "Alright, that wraps up our class introduction. Gather your belongings and let's head to Studio 1, where you'll receive the official welcome, along with the next test."

While a group of girls rushed over to grab the teacher's attention, Nadia swooped in to congratulate her friend.

"What an entrance! Let those brats compete for his attention—he's already got his eyes on you."

"What are you talking about?" Gabrielle said, taking a sip from her water bottle. "He picked me just because I was late."

"Exactly," Nadia said, distracted by her reflection in the mirror. "You should've heard them mumble when he wrapped his hands around you."

"Nadia Costa, you are crazy."

"Yup. But at least I know what I want. I'll see you in the next class, beautiful!" Nadia said, hopping away.

"What is she talking about...? I know what I want," Gabrielle muttered to herself, half-offended.

5

STUDIO 1

*T*he next room was much smaller, with only a single window facing the back of the building. Thick, amber-tinted glass and carved wooden trim preserved its original charm, while heavy moss-green velvet drapes framed the view like a stage curtain.

Studio 1. Maybe it was called that for a reason, Gabrielle thought—one room, one chance, one moment to shine.

A woman moved to the front of the class, and waited for everyone to settle. Her blond hair was swept back neatly, and a hidden layer of violet peeked from beneath—a streak almost imperceptible unless the light caught it just right.

"For those of you who don't know me, I'm Rachel Smith, the school's director. We've helped hundreds of dancers just like you launch their careers," she said, pivoting slightly as she surveyed the room. "So, congratulations on making it through the auditions, but know that the actual work starts now. While you'll learn the science of contemporary dance, you'll also learn a great deal about yourself. Yes, one day you'll taste the thrill of performing before hundreds, but more than that, you'll make people feel what art truly is. That is the superpower you carry in your hands. Use it wisely."

Her posture was as elegant as it was bohemian. She had a dreamy, far-off look of an artist, yet when she spoke, her voice carried the authority of a headmistress. "Dancing needs to move through the broken parts of you before it becomes art. You'll cry. You'll be exhausted. Your body will ache. And yes—you'll want to quit at least once a day. Let me be clear: going deep within yourself will probably be the hardest thing you'll ever do. Be gentle. Find support. Ask your teachers, other students, or the professionals that are here to help you. But please reach out. You're stepping into a world with no easy way out… except through."

Gabrielle glanced at her friend—her fear too obvious to hide.

Rachel continued.

"For the rest of the day, we have something else in store for you. You'll be working in what we call a composition class. It's a collaborative exercise that'll bring you all together for one choreographed piece. Basically, we'll be looking at your ability to communicate with each other, assessing your openness, and seeing how well you fit into a group setting. You've already met your instructor—he'll guide you through this session. Questions before we begin? Good."

The teacher stepped forward, and gestured for everyone to spread out, arm's length apart. Gabrielle watched as recognition dawned on some faces. For some, it was known territory. For her, it wasn't. Her heart pounded violently, making her lungs fight for air. She scanned the room for a safe place to hide.

"Damn it," Nadia said as she rushed to her side. "You have stage fright," she whispered. "Just breathe and try to shift your attention. What your body is really expressing is excitement. It feels like fear to you because you're focused on something bad happening. Instead, channel the energy towards a positive outcome. Close your eyes and take a deep breath in."

Gabrielle closed her eyes. Her shoulders dropped, and the frantic pounding in her chest began to ease. Air flowed in as if she hadn't breathed in hours. When she opened her eyes, Nadia was still there, steadying her.

"Thanks," Gabrielle whispered.

Nadia caught the teacher's attention. He acknowledged her intervention with a nod and continued. "Alright, let's begin with this set of moves. Imagine a tiny ball of energy entering your body, completely uncontrollable. When you get on your feet, take a moment to ground yourself—feel the earth supporting you. Then, let that ball of energy strike again and pass it on to the person next to you. Let your body move naturally. Let's give it a shot. Follow me: five, six, seven..."

The music began. This time the rhythm was faster, sharper, edgier.

Gabrielle couldn't keep up. Despite her best efforts to stay focused, a whirlwind of thoughts battered her from within. *Look how bad you are. You're making a fool of yourself.* A storm raged inside her. The desire to flow with the music crashed to the floor—pieces of her soul scattered across the room. She knew she was off by a few seconds. She tried to improvise, but her legs had a mind of their own. Before the exercise was over, Gabrielle left the room in a hurry, not daring to look back.

Whispers, sharp as needles against her skin, followed her, mocking her retreat. The air itself had the smell of unspoken judgment, pressing in from every side.

Nadia caught up with her in the hallway.

"Are you okay?"

"I need some air."

"Let's go outside."

Without hesitation, Gabrielle stepped into the elevator and went down to the main floor. Outside, she found shelter under a tree. Despite the heat, Gabrielle couldn't stop shaking.

"I don't know if I can do this," she said.

"Of course you can."

"What if I'm not as good as they think I am?"

"Would that be so bad? I mean, aren't we here to learn? And besides, I looked around, and I saw some pretty ugly things. You're not the worst. I think you're a little hard on yourself. It's just your first day."

"I don't want to mess this up, Nad."

"You won't. Now, let's go back inside and let's try to have some fun, okay?"

Nadia stepped into the sunlight and twisted her long hair into a neat bun.

"How do you stay so calm and put together?" Gabrielle asked.

"Oh, boy. We could be here all day talking about it... You know I come from a large Italian family—so things always go wrong. When we were kids, my mother would gather me, my brothers, and my sisters for what she called intervention sessions. Let's just say we've had plenty of practice."

"My dad and I didn't have a good relationship with emotions," Gabrielle admitted. "We didn't have any."

"I see... that explains a lot," Nadia said, offering her hand. "Come on—we should get going if we don't want to be late for lunch," she added with a friendly smirk.

"Thanks for this," Gabrielle replied.

"No worries! Hey, why don't we go out tonight?"

"Could this clean up the mess I'm in, Doctor?"

"Possibly not. But you might meet someone there, and that could help you relax a bit—who knows?" Nadia teased, giving Gabrielle a playful nudge.

6

OFF BALANCE

*T*he café hummed with chatter and clinking mugs, the lunchtime crowd swelling even more than usual in this back-to-school season. Gabrielle barely had time to take it all in before Nadia's boyfriend came sprinting over. He leaped into Nadia's arms, and they kissed, unabashed as ever —something Gabrielle couldn't help but feel uneasy with.

Erick was a proud Mexican boy, many years older than her, yet still carrying the reckless impulses of youth. Short, yes, but his swagger more than made up for it.

From the moment he saw Nadia, Gabrielle could tell he was completely smitten—utterly certain she was the one. She shook her head. Seriously? How could two people meet and feel this much connection? And yet, watching them, she couldn't help but wonder at the possibility.

He seemed to glow with the same fearless energy Nadia had. Funny, charming, effortlessly at ease in the room—they moved together like a pair who had known each other forever. Gabrielle's gaze lingered with a sense of awe at how natural and alive their bond felt.

After releasing the embrace, Erick wiped a dark layer of Nadia's hair from his face.

"Gabrielle! I've heard so much about you—it's really nice to finally meet."

She offered a tight, nervous smile. "It's nice to meet you too."

"Nadia told me you're from the Islands. How are you finding the city so far?" he said, holding on to his girlfriend's waist.

"It's okay. Different for sure."

"Great." He smiled wider than necessary, letting it linger there for a moment before turning back to face Nadia. "So, how was school?"

"Very good. We have great teachers and the classes look promising," Nadia said. "I think we're gonna have fun."

Gabrielle nodded, forcing her own smile, still caught up in the way they fit together, how effortlessly they seemed to belong in each other's presence. She then looked out the window at the bustling street—the roar of traffic, pedestrians rushing by, and the frantic energy of short lunch breaks. Erick was right—the city was a world apart from her hometown. It was chaotic, overwhelming, but then she noticed the flowers blooming in the street garden and the brilliant blue sky stretching above. Perhaps, she thought, this place wasn't all bad after all.

"Well," Nadia said, glancing at the menu, "we should probably order before the crowd swallows us."

The doorbell chimed again, but this time, the man who entered wasn't in a rush. Gabrielle's gaze stayed fixed on him as he approached the counter and ordered a sandwich and an iced tea. No dessert.

Feeling the weight of someone's gaze, he turned, revealing

dark, profound eyes beneath his glasses. Gabrielle couldn't look away.

"It's him," she breathed out.

The man with the digit tattoo.

Erick's phone rang. He quickly looked at the caller's name, and by the look on his face, Gabrielle knew he would need to take it.

"Hello, Erick speaking," he said, before excusing himself.

"Seriously? When will we ever get a moment without that stupid phone?" Nadia said as she pointed to the menu. "Order this for me—I'm going to the ladies' room." She grabbed her purse as if someone were trying to steal it and walked away.

Gabrielle looked back at the man.

A pair of black trousers and a crisp, perfectly ironed matching shirt completed his look. Upon receiving his order, he thanked the woman behind the counter and scanned the room for a place to sit. His eyes landed on Gabrielle, and he lingered there for a moment. Time seemed meaningless as she stared back, unsure how long she had been caught in his gaze. All she knew was that it lasted longer than it should have, for she couldn't erase the glint of his eyes from her memory.

He smiled, as if he knew—and her heart flipped over a thousand times.

As he drew closer, Gabrielle pressed her hands to her lap and shifted slightly in her seat.

"Hi," he said, in a warm, dangerous voice. He pointed to the empty chair in front of her. "May I?"

She nodded with a tilt of her head.

"Have we met before? Your face seems familiar."

Feeling her heart race, Gabrielle wondered if he noticed the blush creeping up her cheeks.

"We met at this counter a few hours ago," she said.

"Oh yes, I remember. You're the girl who likes to stay in bed."

His teasing smile was irresistible.

"Yup, that would be me," she replied.

He tilted his head slightly, adding to his playful charm. "You speak with an accent. Where are you from?"

"The Magdalen Islands."

"Wow, that's not next door. What brings you here?" he asked, eager to learn about the newcomer.

"It's a long story," she said, glancing over to where her friends would be returning.

"I have time," he replied with a soft smile.

Gabrielle hesitated. "I… I have to go."

"But you haven't eaten yet," he said, unwilling to let her slip away so easily. He'd seen the same woman twice in the same day—and for him, that was enough of a sign.

Her eyes went back and forth in search of Nadia and her boyfriend. He understood immediately.

He drew in a breath, lowered his head, and smiled from the corners of his perfectly shaped lips as he leaned back in his chair. His arms looked like mountains begging to be explored, his subtle tattoos… precious maps to forbidden worlds.

Their eyes met again. The intensity of his stare was both startling and strangely comforting.

"I'd love to hear the whole story," he said.

Gabrielle hesitated again. A fortress worth conquering lay hidden behind the darkness of his deep brown eyes. Not wanting to shy away from the invitation, she ignored the warnings in her head.

"Maybe we could meet here again at five?" she finally said.

"That sounds good." He took a sip of his iced tea, grabbed

his sandwich, and stood, ready to take off. "It was nice meeting you, Mademoiselle." He touched the rim of his glasses in a small salute and walked away.

From a distance, Gabrielle could hear the buzz of the city in muted tones. It was as if she was being held under water, her emotions tugging at her balance. But this time, she let herself float with it. While she waited for Nadia and Erick, the waitress came back with their order.

Nadia finally walked up behind her and threw herself into her seat.

"We can share Erick's lunch. He won't be joining us after all."

"Why not?"

Nadia rolled her eyes. "He had to leave. That's what happens when your work is more important than your life."

"I'm sorry," Gabrielle said, then looked down and began pushing food around her plate.

"You're not eating?" Nadia asked. "And what's with the red cheeks?"

"Oh, that's nothing. I don't think I've adapted to the heat yet," she said, wiping a stray drop of sweat from her brow and forcing down a bite.

They finished their lunch in silence, then stood and stepped out, moving through the streets without speaking, each lost in their own thoughts.

Back in the studio, Gabrielle returned to her window seat. Exhaustion hit like a hammer—damp palms, spinning head. The voices in her mind pressed harder, urgent and commanding. Memories of the old lady at the airport struck suddenly, uninvited. True or not, the collateral damage had already begun.

7

WHAT WE DON'T SAY

*A*fter class, Gabrielle told Nadia she'd meet her at the apartment after a quick errand. She slipped into the ladies' room, dug through her bag for a new outfit, combed her hair, and retouched her makeup. Half-pleased, she grabbed her bag and ran to the café.

The tattooed man was already sitting when she arrived. Engrossed in a gossip magazine, he seemed at ease—a sharp contrast to the emotional roller coaster swirling inside her. She hesitated, nearly faltering as she made her way toward him.

He looked up.

"Hey, you're back. I wasn't sure if you'd show up. How was your afternoon?"

She smiled nervously and took a seat. "Not bad. How about you?"

"Good. But I have a feeling it's about to get better," he said, leaning back in his chair, hands behind his head. "So, where were we..."

"Shouldn't we start with names?"

"You don't like me calling you Mademoiselle?" He slid the magazine onto the chair next to him, his eyes sparkling with amusement. "Okay, you're right. Let's do that. My name's Miles. Miles Parker. And you are?"

'You are... not going to fall for him,' she thought. "I'm... Gabrielle. Gabrielle Arsenault."

"Nice to meet you, Gabrielle. I've made up stories in my head about why you ran away from your beautiful corner of the world for the big city. I'd love to hear the real reason."

"I didn't run away—I came here for dance school."

"Ah... A childhood dream?" His curiosity was genuine.

"I've always wanted to be a dancer," she said, wrapping a ginger curl around her finger. "Dancing got me through a lot... especially the death of my mother."

His face immediately changed—like winter air cutting through bones.

"I'm sorry," he murmured, glancing at his right arm.

In that moment, Gabrielle noticed the same hollow ache she'd been carrying all these years. She knew he understood grief—not as a passenger, but as someone who had been there in the heart of it.

"And you? Where are you from?" she said. "I can tell you're not from around here, either."

A subtle smile played on his lips as he leaned forward. "I'd say you're the one with an accent."

She blushed.

"But you're right. I was born in Australia. My parents moved here when I was very young."

"Do you remember it?"

"Yes... a little." He looked around. "I miss the ocean most."

"Don't you want to go back?"

"Someday, maybe. Right now I'm focused on keeping my boss's business running."

"I see. A secure job—great pay, great conditions?"

"Yeah. That sums it up."

"And do you come here often? I mean, to this café."

"No, not really. But I think after today, it might steal the number one spot," he said.

"Might become my favorite spot, too," Gabrielle added, still lost in the glitter of his eyes.

She leaned forward and looked down at her hands—they were trembling.

In minutes, she went from not wanting to get involved to wanting nothing other than to spend time with him. Her thoughts, playing hide-and-seek, left her no choice but to follow her intuition.

"Would you like to go?" he asked, taking the cue.

"Go where?"

"For a walk. Don't worry."

"Yes, I'd love to."

He motioned politely for her to move ahead.

As she stood, his hand lingered on her right hip—unexpected, intimate. She prayed he hadn't seen her face; otherwise, any attempt at resistance would be futile. *I can still run. I can still hide,* she told herself. But his smile, as she turned, let her know he was already in on the secret.

Shoulders relaxed, he stepped forward. Owning the space, he exited the café, self-assured—perhaps even too much so. With each step, the outside world bent to his rhythm.

As they passed a chattering group of tourists, Miles subtly guided Gabrielle closer, his hand brushing her back one more time. You either kept pace or were left behind. Those were the city's unwritten rules. He seemed to have a set of his own.

Gabrielle's head was buzzing. Everywhere she looked, something demanded her attention: bright neon signs advertising unprecedented discounts, small staircases leading to fleeting pockets of exotic entertainment, piles of trash beneath the trees where pigeons picked over crumbs and scraps. In that moment, she understood why she too loved the ocean so much—the steady crash of waves against the shore, the familiar scent of salt clinging to her hair, a rhythm she could trust.

A jarring ring pulled her from her thoughts. She muttered a quick apology before answering.

"Hello?"

"Hi, Gabrielle. I hope I'm not interrupting. Nadia asked me to check if you're still good for tonight."

"Oh... tonight? Right. I don't think I can make it. Maybe tomorrow... if you're free," Gabrielle said, her eyes flicking toward Miles. "Great. You too. Bye."

"Your boyfriend?" Miles asked.

"No. My best friend's boyfriend."

"Ah, I see. So, no boyfriend, then?"

The speed of his questions startled her—yet pleased her in the strangest way. Even though they'd only known each other for a few hours, she realized she couldn't lie to him. Well, she could—but something told her it was better not to.

"I don't have a boyfriend," she said, rubbing her hands down her legs.

"Why not? You're a young and beautiful woman."

A flush spread wide across her cheeks. "Well, let's just say the guys I've met were rather ordinary."

He laughed. A rare, almost childlike wonder sparked in his eyes—a magical light that hinted at a normally suppressed joy.

A line of trees arched over them as they passed.

"What about a girlfriend?" Gabrielle asked, sending the question back to him.

His expression darkened in the shade.

"It's been a couple of years since my last relationship ended. I've enjoyed living alone ever since."

Gabrielle surprised herself with a sigh of relief, a weight lifting from her chest as the tension eased. But the fleeting comfort was only temporary—her reaction to his gaze made it clear that her inner dialogue wouldn't be enough to convince her she had nothing to fear.

"It's getting late. I think I should go," she said.

He raised an eyebrow. "Oh, already?"

"Yes, I'm so sorry. I forgot... I need to practice for tomorrow."

"Okay. You get yourself home safely, then," Miles said, hiding any further disappointment. "It was nice meeting you, Mademoiselle."

He walked away, the wind whipping through his hair, never looking back. Gabrielle watched him go, a confused look on her face. That stubborn streak gave her one last reason to run. As if moving on was ever that simple.

8

WHAT HE KNOWS

*W*hen Gabrielle woke up the next morning, she tossed off the blankets, stretched for a few seconds, then leaned over the right side of the bed to grab her phone. Eyes half-open, she squinted at the screen. Ten-fifteen.

She was late. Again.

She groaned and jumped out of bed. She hated herself for oversleeping—but humiliation was a far worse punishment, one she'd already endured, and she wasn't about to risk another scene. Better to hide in the library. She could invent an excuse later.

By late morning, she had curled herself into a corner between the shelves, needing a few uninterrupted minutes away from thoughts of the mysterious man. Instead, a tensed gasp escaped her mouth as she buried her face in a stack of borrowed books, arms wrapped around them. Would she ever see him again? They hadn't exchanged numbers or made plans, and the odds of another chance encounter felt slim.

Her phone buzzed in her bag. She fished it out and held it to her ear.

"Gabby. Where the hell are you?"

"I'm at the library," she whispered. "I overslept."

"Yeah, I saw that. Tried to wake you, but you were like a dead man washed up on the shore. I told them you were sick."

"I owe you one."

"No problem. Just glad you're alive. Wanna grab some lunch?"

"Yes, of course."

"Meet me at the café at noon," Nadia said.

"I'll be there."

When Gabrielle arrived, she found Nadia seated by the window, wearing a short skirt and a colorful top. Her long black hair rested on her shoulders, the weight promising a comforting hug.

"I've ordered the usual," she said.

"Perfect. I'm starving."

"Yeah, let's talk about that. What happened? When I came back last night, you were already asleep. And why did you skip class this morning?"

"I didn't hear my alarm."

Nadia crossed her arms under her chest. "Seriously? That's the best you can do? Come on, girl. I know you better than that. What *really* happened?"

Gabrielle looked around to make sure no one was listening.

"But don't freak out. I met a guy."

"What? And it didn't occur to you I'd want to know about that?"

"Nad, you always want to know about everything."

"Yeah, maybe, but still…"

"Well, yesterday, after you and Erick left me alone here, a

45

guy came by. We started talking—and we spent some time together after class."

"I can't believe you didn't tell me. Is he good-looking?"

"He's quite something. Mysterious, handsome, tattooed. Definitely not the type my dad would approve of. When Erick called, the guy asked if he was my boyfriend."

"Wow... He's making every second count—I kind of like that. So, when are you seeing him again?"

"I don't think I will."

"Come on. Didn't you like him? I know you're picky, but he seems like a good match—look at you, all giggly."

"This isn't the right time. I only have one shot at a dancing career, and—"

"Blah, blah, blah..."

"Nad, I can't fail this. Seriously—I need every ounce of focus I can get. I'm already in a risky spot, since contemporary wasn't my training. And besides, he's not interested in a relationship."

"Why are you saying that?"

"He told me he was fine on his own."

She laughed. "That guy's got you wrapped around his finger!"

Gabrielle pressed a hand over Nadia's mouth. "Don't be so loud. People are staring."

"I'm just saying... He doesn't want to scare you, so he pretended to be fine on his own... a good way to get your attention."

"That's silly. He seemed honest. I'm sure he wasn't thinking about that."

"Well, believe what you want, Miss I'm-too-naïve-to-see-what's-really-going-on, but it's obvious. And besides, falling in love isn't something you can plan or predict. It just happens."

Deep down, Gabrielle knew her friend was right.

"Now let's talk about you," Gabrielle said, eager to change the subject. "Didn't you say you were working somewhere after school?"

"Yeah. I'm working for my dad."

"Oh, really? You didn't tell me that," Gabrielle said, a hint of payback in her voice.

"You're right. I'm sorry... I just never thought about it that way. There's nothing to brag about, you know. He built his company from the ground up and became very successful, but that also meant we hardly saw him. Made me feel like he loved the business more than he loved us."

"I'm so sorry. I didn't know."

"It's okay. I should've told you."

"But how are you going to—"

Nadia's face lit up. "Miles? What are you doing here?" she interrupted, spotting one of her father's employees.

Gabrielle held her breath, not daring to turn around. When he opened his mouth to greet her friend, a familiar trouble settled in her chest. She spun around, masking her nerves with a practiced smile.

"Hey," she said.

"Hello, Gabrielle," he replied, as if her presence were no surprise at all.

"Miles? Of course," Nadia mumbled.

Wide-eyed and jaw tight, Gabrielle shot her friend a fierce look, eagerly begging for mercy.

With the greetings done, they sat down, and the waitress approached to take his order.

"Surprise me," he said, his eyes locked on Gabrielle's. "I trust your taste."

His tone sent a shiver down her spine, leaving her nearly breathless.

"Careful what you wish for," she replied, smirking at him. She turned to the waitress. "He'll have the special du jour, with dessert," she added.

"Damn, what are you doing to her? Never seen that side of her before," Nadia teased, then shifted to the urgent work questions she had for Miles.

Gabrielle blushed and lowered her gaze to her plate, grateful for the excuse to focus on something else. She nibbled at her food, fidgeting with the fork between bites, aware that he noticed.

"Not into what you ordered?" Miles asked. "Should I be worried about what you got me?"

"She hardly eats when she's nervous," Nadia teased again, a grin on her face.

Gabrielle responded with a swift kick under the table, cheeks warming as she ducked her head.

"Well, I'm off—doctor's appointment," Nadia said. "I'll catch *you* later in class," she continued, leaving Gabrielle alone with Miles.

"Hope I haven't disturbed lunch with your friend," Miles said.

Gabrielle rubbed the back of her neck. "I didn't know you worked together."

"It seems our paths were bound to meet, one way or another."

"I haven't decided yet whether that's a good thing."

"Why's that?"

"You make me uncomfortable," she confessed, watching his smile return.

"I'll take that as a compliment."

"That's not how I meant it."

"Meaning is a slippery thing, wouldn't you agree?" he leaned in just slightly, his eyes teasing hers. "Now that your friend's gone, I take it you've got nothing planned for the rest of your lunch break? I'd like to show you something."

As she glanced at her watch, her arm brushed her bag off the chair, sending it sliding under the table. They both leaned over to pick it up. But she paused briefly when their hands touched, her heart beating faster.

He looked up, smiled, and then settled back in his chair, catching the waitress's attention with a quick glance.

"We'll take these to go," he said.

9

PAPER WINGS

They stepped out of the café into the midday sun. The air carried a golden shimmer—warm but not hot—the kind of day that slows you down and allows whatever wants to emerge to simply emerge.

Miles carried his lunch in one hand. His wallet in the other. Gabrielle dropped her sandwich into her bag and slung it over one shoulder, like a city-dweller who hadn't quite made peace with the city yet.

"Where are we going?" she asked.

He nodded north, toward the mountain. "A place I used to go. I think you'll like it."

"That sounds vaguely threatening."

He smirked. "Only emotionally."

They walked across Sherbrooke Street at Park Avenue, dodging cyclists on duty and art students sketching on the sidewalks—some wearing headphones, others huddled together, humming a Taylor Swift song. Near the park gate, a street musician played soft jazz, the notes floating through the air like dragonflies dancing for the first time.

They began the slow climb up the mountain. The city slipped behind them, its buzz fading in the background. Only the rustle of trees and the occasional bark of a dog remained.

The trail wound gently, dappled with sunlight and shade. To their left, the mountain rose in layers: stones, greenery, and sky. Between the trees, the city peeked through, rooftops and chimneys like curious eavesdroppers.

"The place I want to show you is like a hidden gem," Miles said, his voice low, reverent. "Everyone goes to the lookout or Beaver Lake. But this slope? Most people just miss it."

She looked at him and smiled. "I like it already."

A crow cawed from a branch above, and Gabrielle raised her gaze. The trees leaned inward, forming a lush, leafy archway. Beneath her feet, the path had cracked where roots had pushed through, reminding the pavement who came first.

The trail opened onto a secluded hill, soft grass underfoot. At the top, a weathered wooden bench sat in the shade of a maple, with clusters of red sumac rising behind it, their berry cones glowing in the sun.

Miles pointed. "There."

Gabrielle stepped off the trail, took off her shoes and raced to the top. "First one at the top wins!" she said.

Miles, caught off guard for a moment, quickly followed, his shoes already feeling too heavy.

He picked up the pace and caught up just as she reached the top, both of them trying to catch their breath.

"You got me," he said, giving her a playful shove. "I thought I had you there for a second."

Miles wiped his forehead with the back of his hand and straightened up, still panting but clearly too proud to show it.

"Guess you'll have to try harder next time," she said, her

grin wide and satisfied. "Maybe if you had taken off your shoes..."

Miles bent over, hands on his knees. "Okay... I admit defeat—for now."

Gabrielle sank onto the wooden bench and leaned back, drinking in the view. Below, the park stretched like a green sea, joggers and children dotting the landscape. Up here on this ledge of sky, the mountain felt entirely theirs.

She took out her sandwich, breaking off a piece of bread for the curious squirrels. Miles stayed quiet, watching the light ripple across the grass and the wind sweep the leaves in waves. His face had softened—edges made round by memory.

They ate in silence for a while—the unhurried kind, the kind that comes when trust settles in.

Then Miles knelt, reached beneath the bench and drew out a small taped bag. From it, he unzipped a weathered leather case.

Gabrielle watched, uncertain.

He glanced up. "Ever flown one?"

"What is it?"

He smiled—soft, boyish. "Model plane. Well, glider—if you want to be exact. No motor. Just wind and bones."

"It looks old. You fly this here?"

"I used to. Every day after school." He balanced the wings with practiced fingers. "My brother and I—we'd fly model gliders off this hill, thinking they could reach the moon."

Gabrielle didn't interrupt.

He exhaled—almost a laugh, but smaller. His eyes swelled, brimming with unshed tears. "We thought we were building an airfield. Really, it was just this." He looked down at the handcrafted glider. "But to us, it was the best thing ever."

She looked out again at the clearing, at the way the hill

curved gently, like an ancient bowl holding sacred artifacts. It was beautiful—but what made it sacred wasn't the view. It was the way he looked at it, the way he carried it in his voice, the memories of a boy with a lot on his heart.

"We called it *The Brother Hawk*," he said. "It's stupid, I know."

"No, it's not."

He looked at her, surprised by her certainty, as if she saw something he could not.

"Hawks are fascinating," she said. "Their vision is insane—like eight times sharper than ours. They're usually on their own unless they've got little ones to care for. And when they fly, you don't hear a thing—their feathers just swallow the air, so they just glide. Somehow back then you already knew."

Something flickered within him. Not quite relief, more like sorrow. He stood with the plane still in his hand.

"Come," he said, offering it over to her, his fingers briefly brushing hers.

"You hold it like this—yep, just like that. Now, when I say 'go,' let it ride the wind."

She laughed. "You're serious?"

"Completely."

She waited. The wind shifted. He nodded. "Go!" She released the glider. It lifted into the air, as if it had been waiting for years, dipped once, then caught the breeze again, curling toward the open sky.

Miles whooped softly—something she hadn't heard from him yet. Pure, uncontained joy.

The glider dipped and kissed the grass, and he bolted after it, arms outstretched, chasing the tiny plane as if gravity didn't exist.

When he returned, he paused briefly, catching his breath, then looked at her and fished in his back pocket.

"Don't move," he said.

The shutter clicked. Just once. She blinked.

"Did you just—?"

He was already tucking his phone away.

"What was that for?" she asked.

He tilted his shoulders slightly, the corner of his mouth tugging upward. "You looked like you belonged here."

Something tender bloomed in her chest. She wanted to speak but didn't trust her voice just yet. Instead, she gazed out at the field. He settled beside her, legs stretched out, leaning back on his forearms.

She took a deep breath, not knowing if it was okay to ask. "Do you still come here?"

"I used to, but it's been a while," he said. "Too many ghosts. But lately..." He glanced at her. "Lately, I've been remembering what it feels like to be happy."

A smile graced her face as she leaned in.

"May I ask about this?" she said, pointing to the tattoo beneath his shirt.

He lifted the edge of his sleeve. 45° 30' 54.72" N, 73° 35' 3.84" W inked on top of each other.

"This one?"

"Yes."

He paused.

"Coordinates. They are the exact coordinates of this place," he said. Then, almost as an afterthought, he added, "It's where I last saw him before he enlisted."

"What happened?"

"He never made it home. That's the only thing I've let myself say for years."

"I'm sorry."

"Don't be. He didn't like pity. He'd say I got the better deal. Peace was my purpose, not war."

Gabrielle's phone buzzed. She pulled it out of her bag and glanced at the screen.

"I'm gonna have to go…"

"Yes, of course. But next time, we'll have to do a rematch. Can't let you win too easily—my pride is still bruised."

"There's going to be a next time?"

"There better be."

10

BEFORE THE PARTY

*I*n the studio, Gabrielle went through the motions of her afternoon classes with ease, though her thoughts kept drifting into daydreams she couldn't control. After the last exercise, Nadia popped up behind her, making her jump, a quick intake of breath betraying her surprise.

"Hello, beautiful!" Nadia leaned in, playfully poking her arm—just enough to stir the pot without crossing the line. "Looks like your lunch break did you some good."

Gabrielle tightened her lips for a split second, her brow arching in a 'really?' kind of way. "Nad, you're so lucky I like you," she said.

"You know I'm right."

"I suppose you are."

"Erick and I are having a party at my dad's place tonight. Wanna come?"

"I don't think I can make it."

"Come on, Gabby. I know crowds make you uneasy, but you've got to mingle a little. We've been over this—you meeting new people."

Gabrielle shrugged, sliding her bag onto her shoulder. "I don't know."

"Only this time. I won't bring it up again. I promise."

Gabrielle raised her eyebrows.

"Why don't you meet me after work? We can go to my dad's place together."

"Alright, if that makes you happy."

"I promise you won't regret it." Nadia hugged her tightly and glanced at the clock. "I have to run. I'll text you the address. See you at eight."

"Guess I have no choice…" Gabrielle mumbled to herself. "Now what?"

She slung her bag over her shoulder and stepped out into the late afternoon, sunlight glinting off the edges of the buildings. By the time she reached the apartment, her thoughts had shifted from Nadia's invitation to the familiar comfort waiting for her in her room. Closing the door behind her, she kicked off her shoes and changed from her dance clothes, eyeing the familiar heap on the bed—soft tops, faded jeans, the sweater she always grabbed when she wanted to curl up with a book. For a moment, she considered letting the evening slip by, hiding from the world. But she'd promised Nadia… she reminded herself, tugging a dress from the wardrobe.

After a long shower and a bit of makeup, the evening settled in, and the thought of going to the party hung before her like a small dare she was now determined to meet.

By the time she stepped outside, the city lights had their own evening gowns ready. The stroll to meet Nadia passed quicker than she thought, each step a mix of anticipation and stubborn resolve.

She stopped in front of Nadia's office building and climbed

the concrete stairs, each footstep steady but unhurried, her hands brushing her dress as they swung lightly at her sides. As she reached for the copper handle, the door swung open with a forceful whoosh, knocking her off balance.

"I'm so sorry—I didn't see you. I keep telling my boss we need new doors, but he won't listen. Are you okay?"

The voice was unmistakably his. She looked up—Miles, holding out a hand.

I'm holding on... hoping you catch me, she almost voiced. Instead, she brushed her palms on her dress and straightened.

"No, it's good. I'm fine. Isn't it a bit late for work?" she asked.

"No rest for the wicked, they say. And you? Already missing me?" His grin lit up his face like sunlight pouring through a window.

"Nadia roped me in. Party at her dad's place."

"At what time?"

"Eight, why?"

He straightened the cuff of his button-up shirt and glanced at the time. A smile touched his lips.

"Seven-fifty-five. Perfect."

Before she could even say a word, he whisked her away to the side of the building, pulled her close, and wrapped his arms around her. Against his chest, Gabrielle felt the warmth of his heartbeat, a comforting drum against her own. Miles leaned in, hands cradling her face, his breath brushing her skin before their lips met. The long-awaited kiss felt like a gift from heaven. Even the stars, usually faint against the city's sky, seemed to rejoice as one.

"I've been wanting to do that ever since we met," he finally said, a touch of relief in his voice. "I hope you have a good time tonight."

He lingered just long enough to press one more kiss to her lips before disappearing into the night.

Gabrielle drew in a deep breath, her heart pounding like a car racing toward the finish line. She pressed herself against the wall. Something greater was clearly at work—such perfect timing couldn't have been of their own making, could it? Thoughts of happily-ever-afters rose from nowhere, casting light into the dark shadows of her past. Could this really be possible?

A few seconds later, the door burst open again. This time it was Nadia. She scanned the space for her friend. Gabrielle, still pressed against the wall, eyes shut, savored the remains of the moment—old ruins clinging to the edges of a faraway mountain, much like the fleeting pulse of life stirring within her.

"My God, what happened to you? Oh no, you saw him."

Gabrielle nodded, unable to speak.

"I had a feeling meeting you here wasn't a good idea. I'm so sorry, Gabby."

Nadia set her purse against the wall and rushed to hug her.

"You didn't know this would happen. It's not your fault."

"I should've known better," Nadia muttered, taking a step back. "Wanna tell me what happened?"

"He held me in his arms," Gabrielle said, her fingers brushing her lips. "And then he kissed me."

Nadia slapped her own forehead. "Oh, shoot! There was a hungry shark, and I shoved you right to it! What did you do?"

"Nothing."

"Why not?"

"He sings like mermaids luring lost sailors; my soul couldn't resist."

"This is not good. Definitely a bad idea."

"I can't fight this. Like every cell in my body longs for him," Gabrielle admitted, her voice trembling.

"Oh, Gabby..." Nadia leaned forward, wrapping her in a tight embrace.

Gabrielle rested her head on Nadia's shoulder, letting her breath return.

By the time they arrived at the party, the place was already buzzing—lights swinging, music thumping through the floorboards, laughter weaving through the joyful chaos. Gabrielle moved robotically in the crowd, her mind replaying the kiss they'd shared, each parcel of memory pulling at her like millions of magnets. Her heart thumped to the rhythm of the music, a drum announcing the end of her world as she knew it. Her thoughts spun—Miles, his eyes, their kiss. *I cannot long for a man like this...* she thought.

She lingered near the balcony, letting the night air brush her cheeks, grounding her for a moment—but even then, her thoughts drifted back to him. Every smile, every movement, every glance she remembered anchored her in a pull she couldn't resist—hinting at a night without end.

Back at the apartment, she headed straight for the shower. Water against her skin had always cleared her head, but that night it did little to calm the fire inside. When the water turned cold, she shut off the tap and stepped out.

Mozart padded after her into the kitchen, tail sweeping the floor as she poured herself a glass of water.

"Must be nice, being a dog," she said. "No worries, no heart problems."

She needed no further proof; his gaze—a self-incriminating plea—confirmed everything.

After setting her glass aside, she walked to her room.

Mozart followed, eyes irresistible.

"Alright, buddy. Make yourself comfortable," she said.

She collapsed onto her bed, face-first, then rolled onto her back, one hand behind her head, staring at the ceiling. Every cell in her body buzzed with the music and the memory of him.

"You see, there's something tragic about us humans. Love's always messy. We're either scared we'll never find it, or we're afraid of losing it once it finds us. Why does love have to be so complicated?"

Mozart tilted his head slightly to the left.

"Tomorrow, the sun will rise, and I'll have his memory to wrestle with." Gabrielle growled, the sound breaking free from the tight coil in her chest. Mozart let out an exasperated sigh, flopping his head onto the bed.

11

THE FIRST YES

*T*he following morning, Gabrielle woke up to the sound of Mozart's scratching on the floor. She got up and opened the door. "You can go now, little guy."

She extended her arms behind her head for a stretch. Feeling refreshed and back in her old shoes, Gabrielle was stunned at how easily life had answered her call. Like nothing had ever happened, she danced her way through her morning routine.

Before leaving, she wrote Nadia a note. *Left early. Took Mozart out. See you in class.*

She grabbed her bag, opened the front door and waved Mozart goodbye.

With renewed determination, she breathed deeply, the scent of pine and damp earth filling her lungs, remembering the years of hard work to get here.

Gabrielle entered the school lobby, and the receptionist walked up to her.

"A man came by this morning and asked me to give you this," she said, handing her a piece of paper folded neatly in half.

Gabrielle took it and opened it.

Was up early. Couldn't sleep. Call me. M.

Her heart skipped a beat.

She closed the note. Placed it in her bag.

"Thank you," she replied, failing to look back.

Battling whether she should call him, she stood still. Paralyzed.

"I've made up my mind, so why in the world am I still struggling with this?"

Gabrielle sighed.

Like a dog at the smell of a treat, she was caught in a loop. Perhaps the suffering was the resistance itself? Maybe this—whatever this was—was meant to be lived and experienced. Could she move on only by giving in?

Gabrielle let the entire day slip by before reaching for her phone. By the time she did, she was on her bed, looking out at the red brick wall.

He immediately picked up.

"Miles speaking."

"It's me, Gabrielle," she replied, gazing at her hands. They were shaking.

"Looks like my message in a bottle reached you," he said, making her smile despite the nerves. "I'll be brief as there's simply no other way to put this," he added, his voice tight with emotion. "I can't stop thinking about you. Last night was..." He paused. "You see, I can't even find the words!" He took a deep breath and continued. "What I want to say is that I'd love more time with you. When can we meet again?"

Gabrielle stayed silent. In that moment, a strange lightness swept in. She felt seen. Beautiful. Worst—needed.

The treat was getting closer.

He continued.

"I know a Japanese restaurant we could go to. The owner is a good friend of mine. It's close to school, but since I can choose our table, you won't have to worry about bumping into people you know. What do you think?"

"Are you always this clever?" Gabrielle replied.

"Only with you."

Her eyes crinkled in a smile.

"Alright, show me what you've got," she said, surprised by her own boldness.

"Meet me at Biiru at seven."

"Are you assuming I'm free tonight?"

"Are you not?"

"I have a life, you know. Maybe I have something else planned."

"You're a good kisser, but not a good liar."

"Alright, you got me," she said.

They hung up, and Gabrielle collapsed onto her bed, screaming as loud as she could into her pillow. Mozart immediately pushed the door open and leapt onto her side.

Back to square one.

She lay there for a while, letting her emotions settle, until the late afternoon light faded. Slowly, she rose, changed her clothes, and fussed over the simplest details more than she expected. After a few moments, she finally stepped out into the evening, the city still holding onto the day's lingering warmth.

By the time she arrived at the restaurant, dimmed lights gave the red banquettes a warm glow. The smell of Japanese cuisine filled the air like a savory cloud on a Pinterest board, creating the illusion of a feast in the heart of Japan. Biiru was a nice place indeed. Nestled along City Councillors Street, just west of the Quartier des Spectacles and in the shadow of the St-James United Church, this Japanese bistro offered the perfect spot for an interesting night.

On their table sat a collection of exquisitely well-prepared traditional meals—each dish a unique culinary creation unlike anything she'd ever seen. The aromas rose in delicate waves, both intriguing and slightly intimidating.

She stared. Eyes wide.

"Another first time?" Miles teased before picking his favorites.

She tilted her head, offering a smile that bordered on a frown.

He filled his plate and took a few bites.

Gabrielle stayed silent, wondering about a lot more than she was daring to voice.

"Tell me... what would you like to know?" he said.

"What are you willing to share?"

"Bringing up my brother was already pretty personal. I don't think I can top that. But, since the family door's open, I could let you in on the rest..." His voice softened. "My parents have been happily married since high school, and we did a lot of traveling when I was a kid. Now they're headed back to Australia—not sure if it's for good. They just can't seem to stay in one place. What about you? How's your family?"

"My dad still lives on the island where I grew up. He never really travels—I don't think he ever did. I don't have any brothers or sisters. My mom died when I was four, so... it's just me and him," she said, a trace of bitterness in her voice.

"I'm sorry." He laid down his chopsticks and reached for her hand. He looked straight into her eyes, his palm hugging hers. "I think it gets better with time. But we never stop missing them, do we?"

"I still miss her every single day. I try to talk to her when I can. She knows everything that happens in my life. I..." She paused. "I told her about you."

"Oh, really?" He leaned forward, his eyes curious. "What did you tell her? That you finally met a guy you can't stop thinking about?"

Her cheeks turned red.

"You have way too much confidence in yourself."

"You really match the colors of this place to a T," he said, teasing her. "I love it when you blush."

"You're not making it easy, you know that?"

"Easy isn't fun," Miles answered with a wink. "But please go ahead. I'll try not to interrupt you this time."

"Thank you." She adjusted her hair and took a deep breath. "I told her about this guy I met. Tall, handsome, maybe even a little troublesome. Definitely the kind of guy Dad wouldn't approve of," she confessed, struggling to hold his gaze.

"That's quite pleasing." His lips reached the corners of his eyes. "Tell me more about you. What do you like?"

"Well, let's see," Gabrielle said, her mind still foggy as she tried regaining her composure. "Spring is my favorite season. There's nothing better than losing myself in a dance I've practiced so much I know every beat. And music, of course—it captures emotions in the moments that matter most and plays them back when you need them." She paused, something softer slipping into her voice. "And..." her gaze found his, lingering. "I love it when you look at me. Your eyes make me happy."

"Careful," Miles warned, a smile tugging at his lips. "You're venturing onto dangerous territory."

She smiled back. "And you? What do you like?"

"I like to walk outside when the leaves fall. I love playing guitar when I get home from work. When I was a teenager, I played in our school band. We were terrible, but we didn't care—and I miss that. I also like the way your hair falls wherever it wants. Right now, I'd love to kiss you."

Gabrielle laughed softly, shaking her head. "You really know how to pile it on, don't you?"

Miles grinned. "I prefer to tell the truth."

She leaned back slightly. "Hmm... truth, or charm?"

"Both," he said, eyes sparkling. "And maybe a little trouble too—like you put it so well yourself."

She rolled her eyes but couldn't hide her smile. Her chest fluttered in that familiar, insistent way he always stirred. "You know this road only leads to trouble if you keep going," she teased, her eyes holding his.

Miles leaned closer, lowering his voice just enough to make her pulse skip. "Maybe that's the point."

The clatter of dishes and the hum of conversations faded into the background. In her chest, caution and curiosity wrestled, each tugging at her heartbeat—yet neither strong enough to break the undeniable pull of him.

Trouble, she realized, had never looked so tempting.

12

ALMOST

Saturdays were never this slow. Gabrielle swore the clock had something against her. Every few minutes, she checked her phone, hoping it might somehow speed things up.

After countless outfit changes, she finally settled on a casual red-and-white flowered dress, cinched at the waist, showing the delicate arch of her dancer's back. She'd agreed to meet him at Biiru again—twice in as many days—but the hours stretched between them like waiting for the next *Bridgerton* season.

When Gabrielle arrived at the restaurant, she asked for their reserved spot.

"Mr. Parker isn't here yet. Would you like to wait for him, or I can show you to your table if you prefer?"

"No, it's okay. I'll wait for him here. Thank you."

Retreating behind the line, she watched groups eager to share a meal take over the restaurant, and couples squeeze tables together by the large window for a more intimate dinner.

"Sorry I'm late," Miles said, stepping in beside her. Shadows under his eyes hinted at a sleepless night.

"Are you okay?" Gabrielle asked, watching him make eye contact with the manager.

"Yeah, I'm fine," he replied.

The waiter appeared and led them to their table.

They sat, but the charm of the place couldn't bridge the silence stretching between them. The connection they'd shared the night before suddenly felt out of reach.

Miles spoke first.

"I have to go."

"What do you mean?"

"I'm leaving town."

"What are you talking about?" Gabrielle asked, half distraught.

He sighed. "Turns out I have a son on the other side of the continent. One I didn't know about twenty-four hours ago."

"What?" Gabrielle's heart kicked her in the chest.

"We agreed it was best if she didn't keep it—we had just broken up. I guess she changed her mind and never told me." He ran his hands through his hair, disbelief still clinging to his bones.

Gabrielle's leg twitched, toes tapping out a restless energy she couldn't contain. "I can't believe this is happening…"

"Look, everything I told you was true," Miles said quickly, trying to ease the tension between them. "I didn't mean for it to be like this…" He reached across the table to take her hand, but she locked hers tightly under her legs. He leaned back. "It's been over two years since she left town. I hadn't heard from her until last night—a message on my phone." He glanced at Gabrielle. She didn't look back. "What was I supposed to do?"

"I don't know," Gabrielle said. "Maybe... don't make a child with a girl you don't plan on staying with?"

Miles recoiled. "You were expecting what? It's not like—" He stopped himself, realizing he was stepping right off a cliff.

"Like what?" Her eyes locked on his, sharp as shattered glass.

"I'm sorry. That's not what I meant to say." He looked away. "I knew I'd regret this either way. But... I think it's better if we don't see each other anymore."

Gabrielle wanted to scream. Instead, she blurted a response she barely recognized.

"I could go with you," she said, the words leaping out before she had a chance to catch them.

"Please don't do this. We both know it's impossible. You have your dream here, and I'm... I'm a dad now."

She stood, heart hammering, and walked away.

"Gabrielle! Wait!"

But she was already gone.

She wandered through the streets, letting her feet trace the familiar paths they had walked together just days ago. The corners that once seemed full of possibility now pressed in— sharp, unyielding. Store windows glimmered with her own reflection; the late-night streets nearly empty.

"Why?" she whispered, pressing her hands to her chest as if she could steady the wild beast of her heart.

At last, she found a clear bench in the park. She lay back, gazing at the sky, hands clutching her chest as tears carved silent rivers down her cheeks.

Pain, her most loyal companion, leaned in—unbidden, unwelcome.

13

TATTOOED HEART

The silence of the library wasn't as peaceful as it used to be on this late Sunday afternoon.

Gabrielle sat at her table, staring into space.

Where was everybody?

And her?

She should've been out there in the world, wrapped in the arms of her newfound love. But he had kept his promise—ending things before it was too late.

No words. Nothing. Just the slow, insidious erosion of being left behind. Ignored. Toxic. Destructive.

Her gaze dropped to her unanswered texts, each one a tiny bruise she kept pressing on.

She had to speak with him.

Gabrielle pushed herself up—the rusty groan of her chair echoing her despair—and stepped out into the fading day for a walk.

As she wrestled with her internal storm, the world around her seemed blissfully unaware—carefree faces, families soaking in the last golden rays of summer.

She set her number to private and dialed.

"Hello, Miles speaking."

She sat down on the side of the road, her knees weakened by the sound of his voice.

"Hi... it's me. Gabrielle."

Silence.

She brought her hand to her forehead. "I need to talk to you."

More silence.

"Miles, please. I need to see you. Can you please meet me at the park?"

"Give me ten minutes," he finally said, before hanging up.

Gabrielle turned in circles, trying to shake the anxiety that had been building all week. In her mind, seeing him again was the only solution. At the edge of herself, she wished for a different ending, but their story held the seeds of a future that could never happen. At least, not the future she was hoping for.

Miles walked up to her. "Hey," he said.

"Look, I'm so sorry I left like that..." Gabrielle said, searching his face for forgiveness. "It wasn't the right thing to do."

"No, it wasn't," Miles replied. "I thought about how to tell you, but no matter how I played it in my head, I knew it would break your heart... and..."

Tears in Gabrielle's eyes held still, waiting.

"And mine," he added.

He moved in front of her, took her face between his hands, and dropped a kiss on her forehead. "I will miss you, Mademoiselle."

The tears finally spilled, running freely down her cheeks.

He pulled her in, holding her tightly against his chest. Again, Gabrielle didn't resist.

"Will you forget me?" she asked.

"How could I forget you, Gabrielle? I have your smile tattooed on my heart."

Her heart, heavy with unspoken regrets, skipped a few beats.

"Why didn't you reply to my messages?"

Miles released his embrace and Gabrielle watched him search for the most genuine answer he could find.

"I couldn't bear the sight of your pain, knowing I was the cause. I had to leave and it felt like the right thing to do... end things before we took it too far."

He leaned over and touched her cheek with the back of his hand, wiping the tears he took responsibility for. His eyes lingered in hers, revealing more than words could say.

"Why are you looking at me like that?" she asked.

"I'm looking at what I'll come back for," he replied. "I never thought I'd want to remember someone again."

Her knees weakened, and she leaned into his chest, eyes closed, lips parted. He drew her closer, welcoming the touch.

"Please do me a favor," he continued. "Don't dim the light in your heart. Wherever you are, I know when you're happy. I can feel you when you smile."

As if struck by lightning, Gabrielle's heart stopped. The words... echoing those from her mother's last breath.

She stared into Miles's eyes, letting herself, for a moment, bathe in the love he reflected.

"But how can I let go? It hurts so much," Gabrielle said, bracing for the ache she knew would follow.

"Let your emotions run through you. They have a story to

tell. Maybe the story you're meant to live isn't the one with me—at least, not the one you've imagined."

Gabrielle drew a slow, steady breath. "I'm not sure I know how to do that."

Miles wrapped his arms around her and whispered, "Life has a way of mending hearts. We just have to give it time. You'll get through this, I promise."

"GABRIELLE, I know you're in there." Nadia's knock echoed through the room like a Tibetan bowl struck by a toddler.

Gabrielle painfully gathered her broken pieces, stood up, and opened the door.

"Damn, Gabby. You look like..."

"No one asked you. You can leave," Gabrielle said at the edge of herself.

"I'm sorry. Come here," Nadia replied, opening her arms and wrapping them around her. "What happened?"

"He's gone," she replied, sobbing on Nadia's shoulder. "He's really gone..."

"Don't cry," Nadia said, briefly gazing at the wet halo on her new dress. "Please don't inflict this unnecessary pain on yourself," she added, forcing herself back into rescue mode.

"You don't understand..." Gabrielle replied as she distanced herself. "I love him."

"I know." Nadia sat down on the bed.

"For once in my life, I felt alive. I felt enough... like being me actually mattered," Gabrielle confessed, sinking onto the bed and tucking her head under her pillow.

"But you matter, Gabby. I've never known anyone as

amazing as you. You're unforgettable. Never doubt it. You hear me?" Nadia pulled the pillow up into the air.

"But I thought he was the one."

"Do you know what I think? I think every guy we love *is* the one."

"What do you mean?" Gabrielle asked, sitting up on her bed, pulling her hair back, and wiping the tears from her eyes.

"I believe every person we meet comes into our lives for a reason. Whether for a few days or a lifetime, we are, in that moment, connected with 'the One.' We need them to open us up to the next phase of our lives."

"Didn't know you were friends with Rumi," Gabrielle replied, letting a soft exhale run free. "You sound like a crazy poet."

Nadia laughed in return. "You should try it someday. Feels good to be crazy."

"Maybe one day. But right now, I can't."

"Yeah, well, that's the hard part. They say a heartache hurts as much as a broken bone—triggers the same response as real, physical pain. So for now, we're putting your self-care at the top of the list. Go take a shower, slip into something cozy, and let's watch a movie together, okay?"

Gabrielle nodded. "Could you bake me your special recipe?" she asked, with the corners of her lips slowly curving back into a smile.

"Anything for you, Mademoiselle!"

Nadia's culinary talents could probably soothe Gabrielle's pain for the evening, but never for the full journey ahead. Life, relentless and indifferent, paid no heed to the heartache of broken hearts. Like the fate of seasons endlessly swirling in perfect harmony, she was challenged to keep moving, to embrace each transition with surrender and trust. Yet this road—lined with wounds that never healed and a past she never chose—offered her no exits, no escape.

14
SEASONS OF YOU

Dear Miles,

Despite life's rough patches, I've always found reasons to be happy—glimmers of hope, even on the rainiest days.

But now? I'm afraid I can't see this through alone.

Eight months have passed since you left, and still, I find myself haunted by thoughts of you.

Too many to bear honestly.

We knew each other for what—a week? Two, at best.

And yet, saying yes to that time with you feels like I unknowingly pressed pause on my life.

Now I can't seem to press play again.

Is there a new road I'm meant to follow?

A new dream I need to chase?

Tell me—cause I'm tired of trying to figure this out on my own.

Dance has always been my safe place, the one thing that made the world make sense.

But even this feels too fragile now.

And I'm terrified of losing that, too.

I'm afraid to admit it, but right now, the only thing I want is you—you, holding every piece of me together so I don't fall apart.

I still hear your voice.

I still smell you in the wind, brushing against the leaves of the trees we used to walk under.

I try to run, but the memories always find me—uninvited guests that pull me under.

Every time my phone lights up, my heart turns over a thousand times, hoping it's you.

I am bound to you. And to the memories of us.

I need to know: Do you still think of me?

You said you wouldn't forget.

Remember? The tattoo on your heart...

As winter sheds its old skin, I pray for an escape.

But that would mean letting you go forever.
And that? I don't think I can.
Your words. Your voice.
I'm tempted to replay them in my mind again and again—but haven't I suffered enough?
Teach me how to forget you.
Don't you owe me that, after all?

Gabrielle closed her journal—the scent of lavender lingering from the dried flowers pressed between its pages—then tucked it carefully under her mattress and lay back. A warm breeze slipped through the open window, carrying the sweetness of blooming flowers and brushing gently against her pale skin, greyed by the long winter.

She gazed at the strip of sunlight stretching between her desk and the wide-open sky.

Flowers.

"I need to get flowers..."

She picked up her phone. Sunday, 1:11 p.m.

"Of course..." she whispered, remembering how her dad used to talk about what her mother had taught him about numbers. "They matter more than we think," she would say.

"Maybe numbers do matter. Life's definitely trying to tell me something—I just wish it spoke in a language I could understand."

She stood and walked out of her room, letting the soft breeze guide her down the street toward the flower shop.

Outside, behind the glass storefront, a celebration of colors greeted her eyes—delicate white cosmos, bright purple dahlias, ravishing red and tangerine tulips—all gathered with care, as if their beauty alone could mend a broken heart. She lingered there for a moment, letting the blooms soothe her, before heading back to school, aware that the final push toward the end of the semester was waiting.

She promised herself she'd get a bouquet after class.

Back at the studio, the warmth of the morning sun streamed through the windows. Gabrielle stretched, hands brushing the smooth wooden rail in front of the floor-to-ceiling mirrors. Beside her, Nadia lifted a sun-kissed leg, leaning toward the light as if greeting the day itself.

"Summer's almost here," she said dreamily. "I'm so ready to ditch the coats and boots and walk barefoot in my new dress."

Gabrielle wasn't sharing her friend's enthusiasm. "I'm losing it, Nad," she muttered, eyes fixed on her own reflection.

Nadia lowered her leg and turned to face her. "What do you mean, you're losing it?"

"I'm falling behind. My moves feel off. My hips are stiff, and my muscles are tight," she said pointing to different parts of her body, as if the dysfunction could be mapped from the outside. "And I can't even feel the music anymore..."

"Maybe you just push too hard. Maybe you need a break."

"No. It's not that. I know what soreness feels like. This isn't it."

"What are you saying?" Nadia asked, lengthening the back of her other leg against the rail.

"I don't know." Gabrielle exhaled. "I can't breathe. There's this... rage building inside, and I can't stop thinking about... you know who. I'm surrounded by people, but I feel completely alone. Everyone's leaving. And I think... my spirit's leaving too."

"Whoa, hold on." Nadia dropped her leg and placed her hands firmly on Gabrielle's arms. "Breathe, girl... This is temporary. Your flow will come back, I promise. You just need to process what happened. You've been through a lot."

"Something in me says I can't quit. I have to keep pushing," Gabrielle murmured, her gaze drifting into Nadia's eyes. "But I'm tired. I haven't slept in months. My body wants to stop... I know this is what they warned us about, but it feels like something else is happening—something beneath the surface, pulling at me."

"Baby steps, okay? Baby steps. Take me, for example. I came in wide-eyed and naïve. Now I'm realizing maybe this path isn't mine after all—and that's okay. I still love dancing, but I know I'll move on to something else after that. I don't know what yet, but I'm trusting that little voice," Nadia said, hoping to restore her friend's spirit. "You've got that voice too. I know you do. Even if the road changes, you've got to trust it. That inner GPS—it's all we really have."

Gabrielle's shoulders sank. She fought back tears and glanced around. Nobody had arrived yet.

"I know dance will always be a part of your life," Nadia continued. "But listen—your body is mirroring all the emotions you've bottled up. Let them go, and you'll move freely again. You just have to release the madness running wild inside your mind."

"I'm exhausted."

"I bet you are. So ask yourself—what can you do right now to make things a little better?"

"Disappear?"

"Come on, Gabby. Help yourself a little."

"I don't know… going off-grid sounds appealing."

"Alright, retreat all you want." Nadia shrugged. "You've still got weeks left before the year ends. Just get through it, then use the summer to recharge." She grinned and gave Gabrielle a playful shove. "But if I don't see you actually putting in some effort soon, I'll kick your little ass."

Gabrielle chuckled faintly. "You're quite something. Has anyone ever told you that?"

"Yup. Every day of my life. That's part of my charm, isn't it?"

Gabrielle's expression softened. "I'm glad I'm going through this with you."

"You'll get through this, don't worry. And you'll be stronger for it. Just don't lose sight of who you are, okay?"

"I'll try."

The classroom door swung open, and the first students began filing in.

15

WHITE WALLS

*G*abrielle sat rigid, her back against the metal chair, eyes darting around the room. White walls pressed in, while arrow windows aimed at her like a personal accusation.

A stingy slice of afternoon sun slipped through, doing little to warm the stark, uncluttered space. A clinical smell hung in the air.

Rachel's few possessions were like lonely stars scattered across a night sky—isolated, without pull or flow. It was as if she had built a moat out of thin air, keeping everyone at bay. In that sterile environment, Rachel seemed even more intimidating than the first time Gabrielle saw her. With her blond hair neatly tucked into a perfect bun and a short black dress hugging her toned, hourglass figure, she looked more like a Navy SEAL than a school principal.

"I asked to see you because I want to talk about something that's been troubling me," she said, perched on the edge of her desk, hands resting neatly on her thighs. The look on her face wasn't so much worry as it was discouragement. "When you first auditioned, everyone saw your astounding potential. You had a raw, untouched sensitivity that took us by surprise. I'm sure you have talent, but right now I'm not seeing it."

Rachel stood and walked behind her desk. "What I'm trying to say, Gabrielle, is that it looks like you've lost the flame—maybe even the desire to dance all together. I'm wondering if what you have left is enough to get you through the first year."

The office was stripped bare—except for the wall facing Gabrielle. That one gleamed with awards, far more than she could ever hope to earn.

Ms. Smith leaned forward, hands pressing down on her desk. Her gold bracelet clinked against the hard surface, a sound requesting attention.

"Can you tell me what's going on?"

Gabrielle looked down, fingers tracing the trim of her sweatshirt. "I... I don't really want to talk about it. It's not really about dancing," she admitted, the weight on her shoulders pressing forward. "A rough breakup, we could say."

"I'm sorry to hear that. But why haven't you said anything?"

"How could I? I'm here to dance; I'm not here to talk about my love life." She rubbed the arms of the chair, afraid she had gone too far.

"Gabrielle, listen to me. Dancing is not possible unless you open your heart. You don't have to reveal things you don't want to, but you have to be okay with being vulnerable. Dancing only works if you give yourself to it."

She paused, her gaze steady.

"Right now, you're holding on to things outside of your

control, and it's affecting your growth. Dancing is like a therapeutic instrument, but you've got to let it wash over you."

She brushed a hand over one of the trophies behind her.

"My mentor used to say: resist nothing. Let the movements show you the places where you need to mend. Dance will always be there to catch you, but you've got to let yourself fall first."

Gabrielle nervously tucked her hands under her thighs.

"I know that's not easy to hear. But if you want to keep going with us, things are gonna have to change."

Gabrielle's hands froze under her lap, a quick breath caught in her chest.

"Alright, you can go now."

Gabrielle stood and left, the door clicking shut behind her.

The teacher appeared in the doorway almost immediately, leaning against the frame. "How did it go?"

Rachel jotted a few notes in Gabrielle's file. "It's hard to say. She'll either buckle under the pressure or rise to it."

"Let's hope it's the latter," he replied.

The hallway buzzed with students rifling through lockers and backpacks, hunting for anything they'd forgotten before their next class. Gabrielle slipped through the crowd, heading toward the kitchen. In the corner, a lone chair sat tucked behind the fridge. Sheltered by two massive concrete pillars, she sank into it, letting her senses drift away like years slipping through her life.

After spending her last reserve of energy thinking about what had just happened in the director's office, she closed her eyes and reached for a pleasant memory—a day at the beach, where sunlight hugged her face and the world felt simple. But even that bliss couldn't break through the storm swirling inside her. In that moment, Gabrielle wondered why she had left her hometown.

"There you are," Nadia said, stepping out from behind the concrete columns. "I've been looking everywhere for you. Your phone wouldn't stop ringing." She handed it over.

"I needed some time alone," Gabrielle said, reaching for her phone.

She glanced at the screen: three missed calls. A voicemail, one second long. No name.

Probably Miles. Typical of him—stir the waters, then disappear before the ripples even reach the shore.

She set it aside. Hearing his voice would only make matters worse.

"Are you okay?" Nadia asked, grabbing a chair and pulling it in front of her.

"I don't have what it takes." Her body leaned forward, and her head dropped into her palms.

"Of course you do. What are you talking about?"

"Ms. Smith called me into her office and told me I had potential, but it wasn't visible. What do you think that means, Miss I-Know-It-All?"

"Now, you're being rude."

"I'm sorry. All of this is just too surreal."

"What's real is the pain, Gabby. You can't run from it or pretend it's not there… You have to feel it. Just don't let it live with you."

The ringing of Gabrielle's phone interrupted the conversation.

"Would you get that, please? Or turn it off already," Nadia continued, standing up and running her hands through her hair, exhaling in frustration. "This sound is driving me crazy."

The phone rang a second time.

"It's a confidential number," Gabrielle said, holding the phone like it was a bomb about to explode.

It rang again.

"Pick it up, and you'll see who it is," Nadia said, running out of patience.

Gabrielle picked up, but the voicemail had already jumped in. She waited a few seconds for the red icon to appear. "Another message," Gabrielle said, before bringing the phone to her ear.

"Hello, Mademoiselle Arsenault."

The lady seemed to talk away from the mic. Gabrielle raised the volume.

"I tried to reach... a few times... with no success. I'm leaving you... message even though I... preferred to speak with... in person. What I'm about to... will be difficult..." Gabrielle could barely pick up the words the woman said, her tone coming from a place with poor connection. "I'm sorry to inform you that..."

The woman said the next words—and the phone slipped from Gabrielle's hand, hitting the floor like a brick.

Nadia rushed to her side, scooped up the phone, and glanced at Gabrielle—her face ghost-white. She pressed 1 twice. The message played again.

"...your father was found dead when we arrived. I'm so sorry. I invite you to contact us for the arrangements that must be made. I'm deeply sorry for your loss."

Nadia stayed quiet, expecting her friend to break down any moment. But Gabrielle's gaze remained fixed on the space in front of her, as if nothing had ever happened.

"We have to get back to class," Gabrielle finally said, rising to her feet.

Nadia hesitated. "Did you hear what the woman just said? I don't think going back in there is a good idea."

"Yeah, I heard. My dad's dead."

Gabrielle took her phone back and met Nadia's eyes. "But this isn't real, right? None of it is. Any second now, I'll wake up. This is just a bad dream."

16

STILL ROCKING

The first day of June marked Gabrielle's return to the islands. The flight had left her unnerved again. Every bump in the air made her grip the armrest, counting breaths, waiting for the plane to finally meet solid ground.

Relief washed over her as the green fields of Havre-aux-Maisons came into view. She had come to settle the affairs of her father's passing, yet her eyes immediately sought something else—the old lighthouse she had long ago named *Mommy's Light*. Standing against the wind and waves, it greeted her like an old companion. Its towering strength was proof of the many years it had stood guard, a fortress for her dreams and a shield against her sorrows.

Each day after school, without fail, she had climbed the spiral staircase to the top, just to share a moment with the lingering spirit of her mother—a memory she now held closer than anything else. Up there, high above the world, Gabrielle found refuge from the weight of her days. It was where she reached for the unconditional warmth of a mother's heart, where she searched, again and again, for a way to keep living without her. Now, she realized, she would have to mourn both her mother's absence, long familiar, and her father's death, still unprocessed.

After collecting her luggage, Gabrielle slid into her father's old car—the neighbor had kindly left it at the airport for her. The familiar hum of the engine and the island's bare, open roads slowly eased the tension left by the flight. When she reached the family land surrounding the lighthouse, she parked near the edge, stepped out, and let the wind greet her. She knelt, sinking into the yielding grass she once called home. A sigh of relief slipped free as she leaned back, her shoulders surrendering to the earth.

Hours slipped away and the sky deepened into a breathtaking blaze of fiery orange and crimson red. The setting sun painted the horizon with vibrant strokes, and the waves rolled gently beneath it, signalling that nightfall was approaching.

It was time to go home.

So much had changed since she last stood on this ground —yet somehow, nothing had. The seascape remained her most treasured possession.

Making her way toward the family house, Gabrielle's feet faltered as she approached the porch.

Her dad's chair rocked slowly, back and forth as though her father's hands still held the arms. It shifted just a little, creaking softly—a quiet, welcoming greeting. She knew he wasn't there—he couldn't be—but the rhythm of the chair was too familiar, like a memory so clear it almost felt true.

She watched the steady motion, her fingers tingling as if she could reach out and touch him. The line between memory and reality grew impossibly thin.

"Gabrielle?" John shouted as soon as she made her way up

the stairs. "What are you doing here this early? Is it summer already?"

She stopped and turned around. "I... I wanted to surprise you," she said, exposing a broken smile.

He walked toward her without hesitation. "Good Lord, it's so good to see you," he said. He embraced her, but his hug was nothing more than a chilly draft announcing a lonely night.

Nauseous, Gabrielle stepped back. "I need to go to my room. Just—give me a minute."

His eyes sparkled with childlike joy. "I'll save you a seat and make your favorite soup!"

Gabrielle glanced over her shoulder toward the porch. The rocking chair sat still.

She retreated to her bedroom. The door creaked slightly as she entered. With one swift gesture, she dropped her suitcase onto the floor, sending dust motes dancing in the sunbeams. She threw herself onto the bed, landing on her back with a heavy sigh—a scream threatening to burst free. She cursed the entire universe with every word she could find, hurling her pillow at the mirror above her desk.

After a moment, Gabrielle took a deep breath, stood up, and caught her reflection in the mirror—a tired face framed by the messy waves of her ginger hair.

She quickly twisted the mess into a bun and headed downstairs.

When her foot touched the last step, her heart stopped. Before her lay a scene both haunting and tender: a meal, perfectly set on the dinner table and her father with his hand on the back of her chair.

"Am I dreaming? Or hallucinating?" Gabrielle whispered as she took her usual spot "Is Mommy going to join us?"

"No, I don't think she will," John said, settling back into his seat, eyes bright with eagerness. "How was it? Moving to the city—did you like it? Made any friends?"

Seasick, Gabrielle murmured a few vague answers and then ate in silence, her mind spinning.

The clink of cutlery on the bowl felt louder than usual.

She set down her spoon and looked at her father. "I think it's time for me to go to bed. I've had a rough day."

"Yes, of course. Do you need anything?"

"I'm fine, really. I just need to sleep."

She turned and headed for the stairs. But after just a few steps, she froze, her body unable to go further. She turned back and burst into tears.

"I need you, Daddy. I need you. I need Miles too. But look at me. I'm alone—stupid—talking to a ghost. How am I supposed to do this? Every cell in my body hurts right now. I'm surprised I even have tears left to cry over you, Daddy—I thought I'd cried them all."

"Oh, pumpkin. It's going to be alright," John said, as if his voice were set on repeat. "I knew you'd come back... so I asked if I could stay a little longer."

He stepped closer, his gaze unwavering, filled with something eternal.

"I don't know how long I have, but if there's anything you want to know, give it a shot. I might not have all the answers... but I've met some kind souls here. Maybe they could help."

Annoyed, she rolled her eyes, unable to believe what she was hearing.

"Daddy, you know I don't believe in angels."

"Just stay open, darling. You might be surprised."

"You know how I feel about surprises," she said, with a hint of sharpness in her voice. "Have you seen Mommy yet?"

"No. But they'll take me to her when my time with you is up."

"Why? Why go now?" Gabrielle's voice cracked, pain spilling out—raw and uncontained.

"I'm afraid these questions have no answers. Asking them only stirs more pain. I've accepted my fate, and so can you. You know, I'm happy. I've lived a full life. Sure, I wished for things to be different at times, but my life review... it was beautiful—especially with you, with your mother. There's something about this place we'd fear less if we truly knew what comes after."

"Why the sudden fascination with death?" Gabrielle frowned, fear darkening her eyes. "It's a greedy monster—it always takes the people we care about the most."

"The past year marked a big change for me," John said, his gaze drifting as if he could see it all unfold. His face was smooth, free of the lines of time. "Something came over me—I restored the house and invited people over. Through that process, I met incredible people, and my view on life shifted more in a few months than it had in the past ten years. Gabby, it gave me a chance to rethink everything. I made some changes for my health—well, that didn't quite work out," he said, smiling, "but still. The biggest lesson I learned was how to express my emotions, sit with my sadness, my anger, and all the blame I carried. By detaching from the physical world and the energies held in my past, I finally freed my spirit and let my dreams take flight. Maybe that's why I see angels now. Who knows? I don't think I've answered your question—but I've come to believe that death isn't a greedy monster. It might just be the complete opposite—a chance for us to see life differently."

"How did you come to terms with Mom's passing?"

"I don't think I ever did. But I learned to make peace with the shadows, accepting the darkness they cast and the secrets they hold. The ache is fading now that I'm here," he said, a small smile touching his lips. "Go to my bedroom. On the desk, you'll find a letter to your mom. Read it when you're ready. Maybe in time it will bring you the comfort you're searching for."

Like sand through fingers, John disappeared, leaving only memories and a cold draft.

Gabrielle closed her eyes. She took a trembling breath, gathering the pieces of herself, before moving up the stairs to her father's bedroom.

At the door, she hesitated for a moment before pushing it open. The bed lay smooth and still. The window was open, and a soft breeze played tag with the creamy lace curtains, as if welcoming something—or someone—in.

Gabrielle opened the dresser and found what she was looking for—her mother's favorite scarf, lavender still clinging to the silk. She folded it carefully and placed it on the pillow—a silent tribute to her parents' expected reunion. Though years had passed, she held tight to the memory of their deep, abiding love. You could always tell how much he loved her by the way he spoke of her. Honoring that felt like the only right thing to do.

Now, the letter.

She glanced at the old desk by the window. On its surface sat a few worn pencils, an old copper lamp, and a small picture frame. Inside was a drawing Gabrielle had made on her fourth birthday: her mother, her father, and herself. A soft smile touched her lips as her eyes landed on a detail she had long forgotten: two white wings drawn behind her mother's back.

"Maybe I do believe in angels, after all."

She sat down at the edge of the bed, took the letter, and carefully unfolded the paper.

My dear and precious ballerina,

I'm so sorry. I've been unusually quiet these past few days, deep in contemplation and introspection.

A shift is coming, and I wanted to prepare myself, like we did before you left.

I wish I had done that sooner. But regrets don't matter, do they?

You were my sun, my star, the reason I became a better man.

And even if I'd known it would end like this, I would've done it all over again.

I still see you—on the dance floor, your red summer dress swirling, those worn pink ballet flats a blur of motion, your soft hair wild around your face, that dazzling smile stealing my heart for ten lifetimes.

But more than that, I wanted to take care of you and live this life by your side—each moment filled with laughter and sunlight, a treasure I now hold dear.

I wish I could have returned the favour, saving you as you saved me that day; the memory of you is still so vivid. Seeing the love in your eyes shining like distant stars made me understand: we do not control the bigger picture.

Your lessons about the universe's secrets continue to teach me acceptance and humility.

You should see our daughter. She makes me think of you even more so now. She has a remarkable spirit and a presence that is so soft and caring. I'm glad you stayed around to help me take care of her.

Soon, my love, we will be together, and we'll watch over her.

I haven't told her goodbye yet, but I can hear them chanting. My hand is weak.

I love you, and I cannot wait to hold you again.

John

Tears ran freely down Gabrielle's face, one hand clutching the letter, the other shaking as it rose to meet her lips.

17

THE PRICE OF INHERITANCE

*C*aught somewhere between sleep and memory, the ring of the phone on her father's desk tugged her back. Gabrielle blinked, disoriented, her hand still resting on the letter. She pushed herself up, steadied her balance, and lifted the receiver.

"Hello?" Her voice barely made it out, thin and scratchy.

"Is this Gabrielle?"

"Mmh... yes. Speaking."

"Hi, my name is Ray. I'm... well, I *was* your father's accountant. I'm very sorry for your loss, and I apologize for calling you at this hour."

Gabrielle glanced at the clock her father had finally put on the wall. Almost eight-thirty.

"Can I stop by this morning? There's something we need to talk about."

"Uh... yeah. Sure."

"How about nine?"

"I'll... yeah, I'll get ready," Gabrielle replied, still half-asleep.

She stared at the phone for a moment, then set the receiver next to the base without pressing it down. The click would've triggered a memory she wasn't ready for.

She went back to her room, changed her clothes, and stood by the window, looking out over the land that now belonged to her. The real question wasn't whether she could take care of the land—but what it would cost her. Her dreams. Her freedom. Much like her father before her.

But the thought of leaving it behind felt like a knife in the chest.

Sun rays filtered through the newly formed leaves of the big oak tree her father had planted the year she was born. Trees this large were rare on the Islands—this was probably the only one. The green was still fresh and bright, not yet deepened by summer.

She reached up to redo her ponytail, but her fingers faltered, the ribbon slipping slightly before she caught it. With the elegant curve of her neck revealed, she stood still in the glow, soaking it in. The warmth on her skin seemed to dissipate the pain, if only for a moment.

A sudden knock rippled through the house.

Gabrielle smoothed the blankets and hurried down the stairs. A second knock.

"Hello?"

The front door stood ajar, swinging gently in the breeze. The accountant peeked through the opening.

"Gabrielle?"

"Hello, Mr..." Gabrielle's voice trailed as she tried to catch up with the sudden rush of emotions she didn't expect.

"Call me Ray." He removed his Tilley hat and tilted his head forward. "Nice to meet you."

Gabrielle stared at him as if he were a blank page. Ray

shifted his weight, glancing down at the floor for a second too long.

"Oh—excuse me," she said. "Come on in."

"I'm here because… I don't believe you were given the full picture of what your father left behind." His voice came out clipped and precise, oddly formal against his casual attire.

Gabrielle stepped back. "What do you mean? Was he in debt?"

"Far from it. More the opposite, actually. You know he remodeled the house and turned it into a B&B?"

"I believe so, yes."

"Well, I don't know how he pulled it off, but he increased the property's value by two hundred percent. I've already had a few investors ask if they can submit an offer."

"But… I don't want to sell. This is my family's home," Gabrielle said quickly, the words tumbling out as the weight of it all hit her. She turned away, pressing her hands to her head, as if trying to keep the remaining pieces of her world together.

"Gabrielle, I know this must be terribly hard. That's why I'm not asking you for an answer right away—I want you to think about it." Ray took a step forward. "Just keep in mind that the longer we wait, the harder it'll be to maintain the property's current value. And you won't be able to keep it as a business unless you work here full time. Look, let me give you the whole picture, and then you can decide what you want to do."

Gabrielle nodded.

They headed over to the dining room. Ray placed his briefcase on the table, then opened it and pulled out a file with her father's name on it.

"The house is estimated at around seven hundred

thousand dollars, give or take. If you sell, you'll owe the agent thirty-five thousand, plus the government's share. Then there's the line of credit to pay off and a few other fees. Your father also made some investments—insurance policies, and an account where he kept the money from your mother's life insurance. He never touched it. Since you're the only child, it's all yours."

Ray paused, his eyes scanning her face.

Gabrielle didn't move. Her expression held steady, unreadable, as if her thoughts had stalled midstream.

"Do you have my father's will?"

"I have it right here. Take a look, but essentially, it confirms you as the sole beneficiary of your father's estate. And since your mother's life insurance was left to him and never touched, it now passes down to you. Altogether, you've inherited over one-point-two million dollars."

"You must be kidding."

"No." Ray cleared his throat. "There's just one thing. Your father cared deeply about your dream. He believed in what you were building, and he didn't want you tempted to quit school and live off the inheritance and never chase your dream." Ray hesitated for a moment, then added, "When we revised the will a few weeks ago, I suggested he add a clause. The money is locked until your twenty-third birthday."

"Wow." She turned around, her hands to her lips. "So... Let me get this straight. I have all this money, but I can't keep the house or use any of it for the next few years?"

"It's a tough spot, I know. But the house is a big responsibility—one that needs constant care. And the money? It's there to protect your future, not complicate your present. He didn't want you rushing into decisions that might cost you more down the road."

"Did it ever cross his mind that I might want to keep the house?"

"Yes. We talked about that too. He didn't want you to be bound to a dream that wasn't yours." Gabrielle held her breath. The words barely registered, drowned out by the ache of losing it all.

"You can think it over, but if I were you, I'd sell the house now—while buyers are still willing to pay more. Keep that money invested, and if you play it right, you could live comfortably for the rest of your life, while living your dream."

She nodded faintly, though she wasn't really listening. The pain was too loud, echoing in every corner of her mind.

"I'll just need an answer by next week," he said. "Unfortunately, I can't hold potential buyers off much longer —especially with the bank expecting the line of credit to be settled."

"Let me think about it."

"Yes, of course. Thank you for your time. And again, I'm very sorry for your loss. Your father was a great man. He will be missed."

Gabrielle lingered by the door, her hand brushing the frame as if to steady herself. She watched him turn, open the driver's side door of the rusty Cadillac, and slide inside. The engine coughed, then rumbled to life. Dust rose in lazy clouds behind the tires, settling over the short summer grass—like her own heart, thirsty for comfort and relief.

The engine's hum faded into the distance, leaving only the soft rustle of leaves stirred by the wind and the weight of everything unsaid hanging between her and the empty road.

18

SURPRISE DELIVERY

A few days had passed since Ray's visit. That morning, Gabrielle found herself on the first step of the front porch, arms resting on her knees, eyes wandering across the wide, open land. The world had carried on without asking anything from her, and for once, she was glad she'd let it.

Above, birds wheeled in tight circles, calling out to potential mates with bright, impatient songs. Buds hovered on the edge of bloom, and the grass below soaked up the first touches of early summer dew.

In that moment, the path became clear: selling the house wasn't just an option—it was the right thing to do. Not because she wanted to leave everything behind, but because her dream was calling, and staying wouldn't bring her any closer to it.

She stepped back into the house, picked up her phone from the counter, and turned off airplane mode. Three messages from Nadia—and one from the bank.

She dialed Nadia's number.

"Hey, it's me."

"How are you feeling?"

"I'm okay—if by okay you mean eating cereal for dinner and negotiating with my emotions like a hostage situation."

"Take your time, seriously. Just let me know if you need anything. Seeing you leave like that... it really messed me up. I felt useless."

"Maybe there's something you can do."

"Name it."

"Your dad... he's wealthy, right?"

"Yeah. Why?"

"Well... I might've inherited a large sum of money. It's a bit complicated, and I'd really like some advice. Do you think he could help me figure it out?"

"I can ask. How much money are we talking about?"

"My dad's accountant gave me a rough estimate. If things line up, it could be over a million."

"What? Oh, my God. That's wild. What are you gonna do with all that money? I mean, that's a lifetime supply of handbags," Nadia said, laughing.

"I think I have a better idea... but I need a second opinion. My dad's accountant might be great at filing taxes, but I'm not sure I trust him with life strategy. I don't want to be rude... but the man drives an old Cadillac."

"Okay, fair enough. I think my dad can help. I'll set up a call so the two of you can talk."

"Thanks. I really appreciate it."

"Of course. Anything for my girl."

"Damn, I wish you were here."

"Me too. But don't worry—call me anytime. I could use a few breaks. It's getting pretty crazy here."

A sharp knock rang out—skin meeting wood with crisp urgency.

Gabrielle turned, stretching her neck to see who it was.

A young man stood on the porch, dust on his boots and a sun-faded cowboy hat perched on his head.

"I'm gonna have to go," Gabrielle said, her voice low.

"Okay. But you know you can wait, right?"

"Wait for what?"

"Dancing. I don't think you should come back now, Gabby. You need a break to let this sink in. You said you wanted to disappear for a while—maybe this is your chance."

Gabrielle's eyes flicked back to the door. The man was still waiting.

"I'm not telling you to give up. I'm telling you to rest."

He knocked again—harder this time.

"I really have to go. I'll call you back."

Gabrielle hung up and walked to the front door.

The man looked to be in his mid-twenties, wearing worn deep-blue jeans and a white V-neck. She opened the door.

"Hello—would John be home by any chance? I have a special delivery for him."

"I'm afraid he's not here at the moment. May I ask who it's from?" Gabrielle said, glancing quickly at the piece of furniture beside him before meeting his eyes again.

"Of course. Where are my manners? My name is James. I've been working with John for the past few months. This is a piece he requested. And you are?"

"I'm Gabrielle, John's daughter."

"I'm so sorry, I didn't recognize you."

"I don't think we've ever met."

"No, you're right," James replied, nodding toward the series of pictures on the wall. "I was referring to those."

John had retrieved childhood photos from dusty boxes in

the attic and placed them in pale, sun-bleached frames along the wall.

"How did I miss this?" Gabrielle said. She lingered a moment, fingers brushing the edges. She drew in a deep breath, then turned back to the man in boots. "He's dead."

The words hung in the air like a hammer poised to strike a finger.

"I'm so sorry. I didn't know. When I last spoke with him, a week ago, everything seemed fine."

"They still don't know what happened."

"That must be hard…"

"I don't think any human can ever fully register this kind of pain. It scratches at you like an old record stuck on repeat—and, you know, the more you try to move the needle, the deeper the groove."

He rubbed the back of his neck; his boots shifted against the newly painted deck.

"I get that. By the way, the desk was for you. I'd understand if you don't want to keep it."

Gabrielle stepped outside, knelt down, and opened the door on her right. In the back, she spotted a small handle.

"What's that?" she asked.

"This unlocks a secret door. Your father had something very special in mind—I tried my best to bring his vision to life. Here, let me show you."

James knelt beside her and pulled the trigger. The back panel swung open, revealing a mosaic of broken glass and fragments of tile, leftover pieces from the house's rebirth.

It read:

From shattered pieces

broken, lost, or scattered,
they always find their way back to us.
May we wait for their return
and harvest the treasures they offer us.

"This is beautiful," Gabrielle said, eyes soft, as if she needed a moment before continuing. "You did a great job. I'm sure he would've loved it."

"Thank you," James replied. "Does that mean you'll keep it?"

"Yes, definitely." She stood and wrapped her arms around him like a blanket over someone's shoulders. Her hands slid away, lingering for a moment before she awkwardly stepped back, eyes returning to the desk.

"Let me bring this inside. Where would you like me to put it?"

"Just below the photographs. I think that's where it belongs."

"Alright. With your precious memories, it goes."

Gabrielle paused for a moment, caught between the weight of her grief and the unexpected warmth of his presence—kind, respectful, surprisingly funny. She wondered why her father never mentioned him. Maybe, she thought, that too was part of the plan.

"There you go," James said, stepping back to admire the result.

"Beautiful. Thank you."

"Look, I know you're probably going through a lot right now, but I'd like to offer you something—but only if you're looking for a distraction." He grabbed his hat and pressed it to his chest. "Maybe you'd be interested in helping us—well, me

—at the ranch? I know we don't really know each other, but we might have a few things in common. I love horses too," he said, glancing at one of the pictures on the wall. "And... I lost someone I cared about deeply as well. My wife."

"I'm so sorry," Gabrielle said. "How did she die?"

"There was a fire in the old barn we were planning to renovate. When Maggie went in to check, she got trapped inside. The door never opened again. I got there just in time to get her out before the fire spread, but the smoke had already done its damage. She passed away in her sleep that night."

"That's terrible... I can't even imagine."

"Right?" He put his hat back on his head. "So instead of losing my mind over it—wondering how I could've prevented it and all the 'what ifs'—I'm throwing myself into rebuilding the whole damn thing before summer kicks in. During that time, I need someone to look after the horses while I finish up the barn. They're out in the pasture now, but they can't stay there much longer—nights are still chilly, and the days are heating up fast."

"I'm not sure I'm the right person for this kind of job."

She glanced back at the photo her father had taken—her younger self, maybe seven or eight, beaming beside Sally, a beautiful horse standing loose behind the old trailer they'd rented for that first summer vacation together.

"Don't get me wrong. I love horses. But I'm kind of a mess right now. I don't think I'd do the poor things any good. Honestly, they'd probably come out worse."

James nodded and handed her a card.

"Just in case you change your mind. You'll know where to find me."

Gabrielle looked down at the card. In the lower corner, just beneath his name, was a small line of handwritten script: *Laughing Acres.*

"Have a good day, miss," he said, turning to leave.

"Um... James?" Gabrielle called quickly.

"Yes?"

"Nice name for the ranch."

"Thanks. It was Maggie's idea." He pushed the door open and stepped outside.

Gabrielle watched him go, like the tide pulling away from the sand. She sensed he'd return with treasures from the sea —new stones to collect, chips of plates that belonged to ancestors, fragments of glass smoothed by the current, ready to catch the light once more.

19

A HELPING HAND

Boxes lined the hallway—some sealed, most still too empty to close. Gabrielle dropped another armful of books onto the floor with a sigh, brushed the hair from her damp forehead, and glanced at the clock. Four forty-four.

Hours spent sorting through her father's life—his notes, jackets, and endless receipts stretching back decades. A grocery bag slouched near the door, stuffed with rolls of packing tape and leftover boxes she'd sweet-talked from a tired cashier in the nearby village. Before she could tear off another strip of tape, her phone buzzed.

She hit speaker.

"Hello?"

"Hi. It's Ray. I've got great news."

"I'm all ears," Gabrielle said, starting to sort the books by size.

"You have a buyer."

"Cheese, that was fast."

"They came in above asking."

"Who does that?"

"They didn't want you to consider other offers. They're kind of desperate."

"How desperate?"

"Well… they need the place by next week."

"What? There's no way I can do that. Why the rush?"

"He's a doctor—just got transferred here. His wife's expecting. Baby's due by the end of the month."

Gabrielle set the books aside and paced in circles around the half-filled boxes.

"Do I even have a choice?"

"You always have a choice. Depends on how badly you want it."

Gabrielle exhaled slowly, her eyes sweeping the room. She stood tall, steadied by the decision already rooting itself inside her. This was the right choice. For her—and for them.

"Okay. Let's do this. If this family needs a place, I want it to be here. This house will be perfect for them."

"Are you sure?"

"One hundred percent."

"Alright. I'll have the agent prepare the papers. I think your father would be very proud of how you're handling this."

"Don't know about that—change always made me anxious." She sighed. "Now I just need to find a place to stay… or head back to the city sooner than expected."

"Not sure if it's still posted, but the last time I was at the post office, I saw an ad—someone looking for help with horses. Room and food included. It was called… something like Laughing Horses."

Gabrielle reached into her back pocket and pulled out the card.

"Laughing Acres?"

"Yeah, that's it."

"I'll look into it. Thanks, Ray."

"See? Everything's falling into place. Expect the papers on your porch tomorrow."

Gabrielle set the phone down and let out a slow breath. She held the card a moment longer, then looked around at the boxes, the books, and the too-many rooms waiting to be sorted. She shook her head slightly, almost amused by the timing.

"Alright, Mr. James," she said. "Let's see if your offer still stands."

She grabbed her phone again and dialed the number on the card.

"Good day! Welcome to Laughing Acres; how may I assist you?"

"James. It's me—Gabrielle."

"Oh, hello! To what do I owe the privilege of your call so soon after our brief, but memorable, encounter?"

"I wanted to know if your offer's still on the table."

"Which one?"

"You only voiced one."

"Right. Which one was that again?"

She chuckled. "I need a place to stay. I just sold the house and have to be out in a week."

"Dear Lord, that was quick."

"Trust me, I'd love a breather. But it doesn't seem to be in the cards."

"Well, I'd be more than happy to welcome you," James replied.

"And—if I may—I need to push my luck a little further," she said.

"Shoot."

"Would you be willing to help me pack up my dad's things? I found a storage facility, but I don't have a truck… or a second set of hands."

"You're in luck. I've got the truck, and I can bring the extra set of hands too. When do we start?"

"I'm already done with his bedroom. Now, I'm in the library. Boxes are getting a little heavy."

"Let me grab dinner, and I'll be right over."

"Oh—you don't have to do that."

"The ad said food included, right?"

Gabrielle laughed.

"Okay then."

She ended the call, letting her last words linger on her smile, then picked up the tape gun, clicked it into place, and stretched her arm over the box to seal it—one box down, one step closer to moving forward.

20

RED DRAGON

James arrived thirty minutes later with a reusable container filled with homemade chili, warm pita bread wrapped in a dish towel, and a thick slab of salted butter.

Gabrielle raised an eyebrow. "You cook too?"

"I feed horses. Same principle—big appetites, no time for fancy."

She smirked. "That's five stars compared to my student meals."

"Figured you'd need something warm and filling. Good fuel to keep us going."

"Thoughtful. Thank you. It smells amazing."

She sat cross-legged in the middle of the living room. James handed her a bowl, and the scent of chili drifted through the room. They cleared the space, settled in, and, spoon in hand, began sorting the books one by one.

"Umm... *Red Dragon*?" James said, turning the book over. "Wouldn't have guessed your dad was a crime thriller kind of guy."

"Oh no, that's not his," Gabrielle replied. "It belonged to my mother. Not sure why she had it. I never read it." She gave a small shiver. "Honestly, I got scared just reading the line on the back."

James slipped into a theatrical tone as he read aloud: "Red Dragon is an engine designed for one purpose—to make the pulse pound, the heart palpitate, the fear glands secrete."

Gabrielle's lips hinted at a smile. "No. Below. The warning."

He dropped back into his natural voice.

"If you're subject to nightmares, don't read it."

"Yeah. That one."

James's curiosity flared. He turned the book over and cracked the cover open.

Something slipped out: an old piece of paper and a faded photograph, held together with a thin red ribbon—the same color as the one tied in Gabrielle's hair.

"Huh… I have a feeling your mother didn't want this lost," James said, holding it up for her to see.

"She knew I'd never open that book. What is it?"

Gabrielle untied the ribbon and lifted the photograph. A woman sleeping on an outdoor mattress at the edge of a forest, sunlight brushing her face. On the back, in shaky handwriting, a date: August 8th, 1977.

Gabrielle whispered, her words trembling: "This would be you… Mommy."

Carefully, she unfolded the letter.

My Sweet Pumpkin,
Nothing about this day is accidental. If you

are reading this now, it's because the moment has finally found you. Let me explain.

You see, in my youngest years I was offered to carry a prophecy. I've been given the opportunity to walk paths beyond the straight line we believe time to be. From there, I have witnessed what was, what is, and what still lives just beyond reach. I understood why you would be mine—even if our lives only brushed against one another for what felt like a few seconds.

Here's the prophecy I was given:

"What was entrusted to start
could not end with the one who started it.
Another hand was always required."

You are the other hand. You were the bridge; the crossing point. I was meant to open the way and you were meant to see it through.

Answers will come, I promise—at the perfect time, as they must. Until then, let me comfort you with this: everything is connected—threads in a vast and sacred tapestry. What touches you echoes beyond you. It reaches others, and through them, the entire universe is transformed, rippling back to you in an endless loop.

From where I stand now, surrounded by

those who have walked before us, I feel it more clearly than ever.

You may wonder how I could speak to you from here.

In truth, your father helped. He channeled my words onto paper—some meant for him, others meant for you.

Beside the book Red Dragon, you'll find my Field Notes bound in old leather—notes gathered from the places I visited.

Do not be deceived by the blank pages.

They are not.

Do not be tempted to write on them—for they are already full.

Gabrielle looked up at James.

"Do you see a worn leather traveler's notebook somewhere near *Red Dragon*?"

He scanned the shelf, then carefully pulled out a well-worn leather notebook. "Is this what you're looking for?" he asked, holding it out to her.

Gabrielle nodded and took the notebook in her hands, feeling the rough leather under her fingers. She flipped through the pages—empty as a coffee mug after a sleepless night. She frowned, unsettled, intrigued, and kept reading.

I will return in time. But until then, know this: I've always been with you.

Helping you reach for dreams you don't even know you carry. I love you. I think of you every day. And don't worry—when the time comes, it will all make sense.

Gabrielle turned the paper and read the P.S., mumbling the words under her breath as they sank in. Her eyes stayed on the last line, sensing James leaning in, curiosity growing.

"May I?" he asked.

She held the note out toward him, hesitating for just a moment, then let her fingers fall away as he took it. He read aloud:

P.S. If you ever travel to that beautiful place before I get the chance to tell you about it, find the small shed first. You'll recognize it easily: black, no windows, only one door. Go inside. There, you'll find a treasure only you can see. Keep it with you—no matter what. It will protect you and those you love.

With grace, Charlotte, your beloved mother.

Her gaze lifted, and she saw James remain still, eyes steady, as if he knew not to break the spell. As if some part of him had been waiting for this moment too. Everything hung suspended—two souls tethered to a mystery just beginning to unfold.

21

EVERYTHING MEANS SOMETHING

*H*er last week at the house went just as expected —too little sleep, too many boxes, and tears triggered by the most ordinary things: plates still tucked in their original box, waiting for a special occasion that never came; a bird hovering on a branch a second too long, as if staring straight into her soul; and the echoes of the last movie they'd watched together, still lingering in the walls of the living room.

Then the questions came—piling up like unopened final-notice letters on the kitchen table: *What truly happened to her father? Why death at all? Why now?*

Were we just supposed to accept it? That life, in all its randomness, handed each of us a different expiration date? Some of us, milk in the fridge—spoiling before the week ran out. Others, canned goods: built to last a hundred years. But what she didn't see coming hit harder than a delivery truck veering across lanes without warning.

It wasn't just one life event or a color-loaded conversation with a friend—it was every single moment. Every breath the wind took seemed to whisper a cruel truth: this could be her last one.

Hypervigilance, she realized, wasn't sustainable. Nor was it something you'd wish on anyone. The human brain is clever, doing what it can to protect us—but it wasn't built for this: the sudden realization that mortality isn't a concept. It's a sure thing.

Some people get a gut-punch epiphany and change everything overnight. Gabrielle didn't. Instead, the world shifted around her—colors grew sharper, sounds clearer, tastes deeper. Not metaphorically. Literally—like the early-morning glow on kitchen tiles, the rough rattle of an old zipper, the whoosh of bird wings swinging past the open window, and the taste of water after crying for too long.

Sensing the fragility of life felt like touching newly formed ice on the edge of a lake in early December—thin, delicate, too fragile to hold one's reflection. *You're still here,* she heard. *You're still here.*

By the end of the week, Gabrielle was ready to move out. She'd packed away the last of her father's belongings—some sent to James's ranch, the rest tucked away in *Maison Papier*, a storage facility in Havre-Aubert, twenty-five miles south of the home she was leaving behind.

The house was now clean, breathing hope again—like a forgiving heart ready to beat fresh new stories. As she glanced at the empty room, a profound knowing settled into her chest. She knew she was honoring her father's dream while stepping boldly into her own—meeting her mother somewhere in between.

Gabrielle imagined the next family arriving, wrapped in the serendipity of a history woven with love, care, and a touch of magic. Life hadn't spared them their struggles, but beyond it all, they had lived deeply—and well. That alone was worth appreciating.

She closed the front door, locked it, slipped the keys beneath the doormat, and packed her luggage into the back of her father's car—just as her mother had done years before.

She drove down the sandy trail that led to the main road. Windows down, rock 'n' roll pulsing through the speakers, she turned north onto Route 199—*Chemin Principal*, as the locals called it. The road stretched like a ribbon over the sandbars, linking one island to the next, skimming between sea and sky. Fifty-five miles of possibility ahead.

Her heart held onto gratitude as much as it could as she left Havre-aux-Maisons. This bare island, dotted with colorful houses blooming like daisies in spring, had been her sacred sanctuary all her life. And now, it seemed, life was nudging her in a different direction.

As Gabrielle drove further, the landscape began to shift— flat fields turned into rocky shores, and small, weathered houses appeared at the curves of the road. The ocean came and went beside her, first on one side, then the other, like a loving passenger keeping her company. James's place was about thirty minutes away.

Pulling into the streets of Old-Harry, Gabrielle spotted the place James had mentioned: Grandma's Bakery—a local favorite for good reason. The warm scent of fresh bread and cinnamon wrapped around her as she stepped inside. She wandered past the display cases, letting her fingers brush the jars of jam and honey, each one more tempting than the last. For a moment, she almost forgot why she was there, caught in the simple pleasure of small-town charm. Then, reminded by the note tucked in her pocket, she moved toward the counter and asked for the bag James had reserved: a few croissants, still warm from the oven.

Back in the car, she carefully unfolded the note. It read: *At the bakery, continue just a little further, then—before the curve—turn right onto Head Street. Follow the sandy trail to the edge of the land. The house will be waiting for you. See you soon.—James*

She slipped the note back into her pocket, her fingers brushing the fabric as if sealing a promise. She got back in the car and drove on, letting the road guide her. Soon, the gravel driveway appeared, flanked by wildflowers swaying in the breeze—she had arrived.

Standing tall and proud, the ranch wore a deep navy-blue gown that shimmered against the turquoise sea. It was a two-story cottage with wide windows framed in crisp white trim. On the porch, a hand-carved bench—weathered just enough to feel loved—and beneath it, a pair of rain boots, neatly tucked away.

Gabrielle parked to the side of the house, sunlight glinting off the hood like a warm welcome. She had spent her whole life breathing the air of her own corner of the islands—and never imagined it could be different just a few miles away.

But this place felt like it belonged in another world.

Barefoot, she walked to the edge of the land, where the horizon stretched like an eternal exhale, and opened her lungs wide. The breath of life. The pull of the current. The depth of the wind. She took it all in.

"Gabrielle!" James's voice cut through the wind like an arrow finding its mark. He'd heard the roar of the old car and came down to meet her. "I'm so glad you're here," he said. "Not too hard to find, I hope?"

He looked every bit the country boy—hat low over his brow, tight white shirt, ripped blue jeans, dark brown boots.

And with that smile—just a little crooked—it was easy to think he might be the sweetest man around.

Gabrielle smiled. "This place is just... breathtaking."

"Isn't it quite something?" he said, glancing toward the horizon. "I never get tired of this."

"Who would..."

"Alright, let's get you settled in. I made lunch—you must be starving."

"Took every ounce of me not to eat those." She handed him the bag of croissants as they headed toward the house.

"The best in the world," he said.

Once inside, Gabrielle followed him, her eyes drifting toward the kitchen window. Through the glass, she caught a hint of the garden and the stretch of land beyond—a fleeting glimpse that hinted at the adventures ahead.

He led her up the staircase. Three doors faced one another, a small welcome centerpiece anchoring the middle. Following his lead, Gabrielle stepped into the second bedroom. Fresh-cut lilies bloomed in an old crystal bowl, soft linens lay neatly pressed on the bed, with an extra quilt folded at the foot. Even a candle waited, dozing on the desk beneath the open window.

"I don't know what to say, James. This is... way too much!"

He laughed and rubbed the back of his neck, sheepish. "Maybe I went a bit overboard with the flowers, huh?"

"Oh no, it's perfect," she said, a smile tugging at her lips. "I might just never want to leave."

"Take your time. Whenever you're ready, I'll be downstairs."

Her heart gave a small lurch—he hadn't caught it, hadn't heard the part that meant more than just the room.

"I'll be down in a few minutes," she said instead, tucking the meaning away for next time.

She unpacked her clothes into the wardrobe, lined her makeup along the desk beneath the window, then glanced down to see James in the yard, gathering the horses for their meal. She slipped on her jacket and headed downstairs.

Shortly after, James stepped in, one hand in the bag of croissants, the other pushing the door open.

"Saw you sneaking a bite!" Gabrielle called, sliding a chair back and settling in.

"How long have you been standing there?"

"Long enough to catch you red-handed."

"Told you they were the best..."

"Well, I forgive you—this time."

He pulled out the last pastries with a sly grin. "They wouldn't survive the night, anyway. Here—those are for you."

"Thanks. So... how long have you been living here?"

"Going on five years. Spent a couple of years in London— that's where I met my wife... well, ex-wife now, I guess. We met in college—me studying architecture, her in a master's for education. That summer, we came to Canada... and never left. We quit school, started working in the village—cutting wood, learning to fish. Funny, since neither of us had ever even held an axe or a fishing line before. Eventually, we saved enough to buy this little piece of paradise."

"And... what happened with architecture?"

"It kind of went on the back burner. Well, technically, I decided not to carry on with it," he said, setting a tray of early garden greens—spinach, radishes, and chives—in the center of the table. "But a year after Maggie passed, I felt ready to jump back in. Funny thing—that's when I met your father. I posted ads here and there, offering renovation services while I learned the ropes. He called a few days later, and I started working for him right away." James looked up. "I've always had a deep respect for the heritage of a place like your family home. Restoring that house... it felt like being part of something bigger than myself—a real blessing."

"I think you did a wonderful job. Unfortunately, I never really got to know that side of him," she said, taking a bite of the homemade dinner: roasted root vegetables—carrots and beets from last fall's harvest, still sweet from months tucked away in the cellar. Beside them, a simple lemon-thyme chicken —crisp on the outside, juicy at the center.

She chewed slowly, letting the warmth settle in her chest.

"James... You really are a wonderful cook."

"Thanks," he said, rubbing the back of his neck again— honest, a little in awe. "I've loved it since I was a kid. My mom let me join her in the kitchen—but I wasn't much of a cook back then... mostly I just sampled everything. Still, I was hooked."

James leaned back in his chair, glancing over his shoulder through the kitchen window. Low, wind-brushed grass sloped gently toward the cliff, the sea beyond catching the last light, gold flickering where the waves met the rocks. The sky was shifting—soft purples bleeding into burnt orange; the horizon exhaling one final breath. Yet he wasn't ready to call it a day.

"Are you done?" he said.

"Yes, thank you. It was delicious."

"Why don't we go outside before the sun sets completely? I'll show you where the horses are. We kinda have an evening ritual."

As she shifted in her seat to stand, his eyes flicked down briefly—catching a glimpse of her thighs. A thought sparked and died before it could grow. *The horses, James. The horses!* He turned back, forcing his gaze upward. "I... I meant to tell you —you might want to change first."

Gabrielle glanced down at the dress she wore, met his eyes, and understood.

"I'll go do that now."

Left alone, James's thoughts spun. *Come on, man, don't go there. You didn't ask her here to hit on her. Pull it together. Be a decent man.*

Before James's thoughts could settle, Gabrielle hurried down the stairs in light blue jeans and a fitted white t-shirt.

"Better?"

"Much better. Now you look like someone the horses might actually let near the fence."

"Ah-ah, funny..." she teased, a smile tugging at her lips.

James led her toward the temporary shelter. He reached the trough first, kneeling to check the water level, his fingers brushing the cool surface to make sure it was just right.

"First thing," he said, "always make sure they've got fresh water after eating. Horses drink a lot." He dipped his hand into the water, then motioned her over. Gabrielle knelt beside him, watching closely.

"See? If it's low or dirty, you clean and refill it. They won't drink if it's stale."

Next, he moved toward the stalls, grabbing the pitchfork.

"Cleaning up the stall is key. You don't want them standing in their own mess overnight—that's how they get sick or uncomfortable."

He scooped out fresh bedding, then handed her the fork. Gabrielle mimicked his motions, the roughness of the straw scraping against her fingers.

"Grooming comes after, like a little treat for both you and

the horses. It keeps them clean and helps you spot any cuts or other issues. Plus, horses love the attention."

He pulled a brush hanging from the wall and handed it to her. She ran it gently over a chestnut mare's coat, feeling the warmth beneath.

James stayed nearby, his gaze following her as she worked.

"Oh, and last thing—always check gates and fences before sunset. Keeps everyone safe."

He locked the barn door behind them and caught her gaze. "There's a rhythm to it. Caring for horses—it's about patience, respect, and being present. You'll be good at this."

A faint pink crept across her cheeks. She looked away for just a moment before meeting his gaze again.

"Thank you for being so kind," she said.

He smiled, and she caught something in his eyes that made her pulse rise—anticipation, or maybe nervousness. Maybe both.

AN UNEXPECTED VISITOR

A month and a half had passed, and the rhythm of the ranch had worked its way into her—into her muscles, her breath, the dirt under her fingertips. Mornings no longer felt cruel, and the tasks James had assigned—feeding, grooming, and mucking out the stalls—no longer felt like chores. She moved through them with ease, surprised by how much she enjoyed the repetition, the lack of pressure, and the absence of perfection needed to feel a sense of purpose. She hadn't realized until now how much work went into caring for a place like this, how much attention it demanded—and, strangely enough, how much peace it gave back.

That morning, Gabrielle caught glimpses of James working on the last section of the barn the fire had destroyed—shifting his weight, tools clinking, muttering under his breath. From the corner of her eye, she noticed him glancing over his shoulder, distracted, as if something or someone kept tugging at his attention.

A black BMW slid into the driveway, kicking up a veil of

dust behind it. The driver could only be James's brother—same jawline, same shoulders, but with the city written all over him. The sudden noise sent a horse to paw at the ground; Gabrielle leaned close, resting a hand on its shoulder, grounding both of them. On the roof, James lurched, grabbing for balance as his brother flashed a triumphant grin.

In the passenger seat, a young girl—maybe twelve, thirteen —rested her head against the window. She looked half-asleep, her attention likely fixed on a device on her lap.

James climbed down, his movements tight with deliberate heaviness as he closed the gap between him and the car.

"Hey. Always making a show, huh?" he said.

"Always the most fun. And better looking too, obviously."

"Yeah, sure," James muttered.

Gabrielle wiped her hands on her jeans and made her way over to James.

"Oh, I see you've got company." James's brother jabbed him in the stomach, leaning in with a hand over his mouth. "No wonder you've been so distant."

James's eyes locked on him, a silent warning blazing: *Don't be stupid—or you'll regret it.* He eased his gaze and looked back at Gabrielle, shifting into a proper introduction.

"Mark, this is Gabrielle. Gabrielle, this is Mark, my brother."

"Nice... to meet you," she said, hesitating. Her pause brought James strange comfort—he was never the one who got away with the girl. The only exception had been his wife.

"The pleasure's all mine," Mark said, taking her hand and dropping a quick kiss on top. He straightened and turned to James. "So... I need you to handle something for me."

"What now?" James asked, lifting an eyebrow, bracing for another one of his impossible stories.

"Well, I got thrown into this enormous project, and I need to be out of town for at least a week," Mark said, sounding mildly annoyed. "Since her mother's not returning my calls, I'm out of options. I need you to check in on her for a few days. I'm sure you can put her to work—cleaning the house or whatever you've got going on here," Mark said, already heading back to his car.

"You could've just called, you know. Not like I have a choice now."

"You're the best. I owe you one," he said, bright smile and a hand on the passenger door. "Hey, baby girl. You're gonna spend a few days at Uncle Jay's," he added. The girl climbed out, eyes glued to her phone.

"Hey Alison. Wow, you've grown so much since the last time I saw you," James said, awkwardness slipping through before he could stop it.

"Hey," she replied, voice flat, like pancakes without syrup.

"So... I'll be back in a few days—you won't even notice I'm gone," Mark said, planting a quick kiss on the top of her head. "Here's her suitcase. Pretty sure she's got everything she needs. See you in a week." He hurried to his car and sped off, leaving a cloud of dust behind.

James scrubbed a hand over his face and mumbled to himself, "Now what?"

Gabrielle moved in, forcing a smile at the girl. "Want to come help me with the horses?" she asked.

"Yeah, okay," Alison mumbled, still staring at her phone, her feet reluctantly shuffling forward.

Gabrielle shot James a look and mouthed, *Charming.*

He mouthed back, *Thanks for that.*

On tiptoe, Gabrielle caught up to her. "I'm Gabrielle, by the way."

Alison stopped and looked up.

Under the brim of her baseball cap, sharp blue eyes stared at her. Messy, frizzy blond hair framed a face that said: stay back. Baggy green pants and a faded grey sweatshirt hid her figure. If there was any doubt, those eyes made it clear—she didn't want to let anybody in.

Gabrielle looked down and walked to the old barn. She wondered how close the girl had been to James's wife—and if bringing her here was the right thing to do. She trusted her gut and kept walking.

"Where are we going?" Alison asked, irritated. "It stinks."

"I want to show you something," Gabrielle said, unbothered by the smell. "See that horse over there? She got here a few days ago but just won't hang out with the others. From where she stands, she's not missing much—she can still see the land around her. But from here? She's missing out on a lot. If she keeps hiding in the shade, the sun can't reach her. All she needs is a little nudge to take a few steps the other way—then maybe everything will change. What do you think?"

Alison shrugged, eyes still flicking to her phone. "What if she doesn't want to be in the sun?"

Gabrielle smiled gently. "Sometimes all it takes is someone showing us it's okay to try."

Alison looked up, a small spark of hope flickering in her eyes.

"Yeah, maybe... What's her name?"

"Mindy."

"Mindy—that's a beautiful name."

Without hesitation, Alison slid her phone into her back pocket, climbed onto the wooden bench, and swung herself over the fence.

The horse took a step back.

"Careful, Alison…" Gabrielle warned.

"It's okay… I've got this." Alison turned back to the horse and took a few careful steps closer, her hand stretched out.

"I get it," she said, looking into the horse's eyes. "I don't like doing stuff I don't want to do either."

Mindy stepped forward.

"There you go."

Alison stood close enough to catch Mindy's uneven breaths. Slowly, she reached out, resting her hand against the side of the horse's head.

"We'll go together, okay?"

Mindy's breath slowed down. Her muscles softened, and her eyes closed halfway. Then, Alison gently led her into the sunlight.

"You see? Not that hard after all," Alison said. "You're a brave girl."

Gabrielle glanced over her shoulder to find James watching from the rooftop. His lips mouthed, *Thank you*—once more— as he gave a small, grateful bow.

That night, Gabrielle slept like a child, the sun's warmth still lingering on her face, a tiny victory resting in her heart. Somehow, she knew that no matter what storms might come next, she could always return to this place within herself— where flowers bloomed all year, and where kindness could shift the course of someone's life, as well as her own.

23

DANCING WITH THE TRUTH

*G*abrielle's long, ginger-tinged hair clung to her neck, thick and sticky; her clothes streaked with dirt and hay—country life in full display. She would need at least two, maybe three washes to get the stains out. But she didn't care. For the first time in a long time, she felt something close to true joy. Bliss.

After an early-evening shower, she slipped into a mossy green dress that made her leaf-colored eyes stand out even more. She wandered outside, crossing to the other side of the land to watch the sun sink into the ocean. Her damp hair clung in heavy, glistening strands that swung with the wind—and her worries, light enough to float away, danced along with it. She twirled through the grassy fields, the last rays of sunlight catching the edges of her dress, and caught herself laughing again—reconnecting with the spirit she thought she'd lost. Golden dust shimmered across the landscape as she spun faster, every cell in her body bubbling with excitement and energy.

From the kitchen window, James watched. He hadn't seen anything this beautiful in a long time. "Would you forgive me... for wanting to love again?" he whispered.

"Who are you talking to?" Alison asked, stepping into the kitchen.

"Eh, nobody," he said, eyes darting toward the window then flicking back just as fast. "I was just singing a song. Humming a tune, you know."

Alison moved in closer.

"What are you looking at? Are you spying on Gabrielle?"

"No, of course not. I was just getting us ready for dinner and... well, she happened to be there."

"Yeah, right. You've got a thing for her... it's all over your face."

"No, I don't. Even if I did—which I don't... grrr... it doesn't matter. It's too late..."

"Too late for what?"

"She's leaving in a few days, remember?" James's jaw tightened, a weight in his voice.

"So, you do have a thing for her."

James gazed out the window, eyes tracing the horizon.

"It's not that simple."

"There's always room to try," Alison said, slipping past him, pushing open the screen door and running outside.

James watched as Alison reached for Gabrielle's hands. Together they ran toward the cliff, chasing the birds into flight, their laughter lifted by the wind as the sun sank low, painting the sky in fire and gold. He gathered the meal and took his turn pushing the screen door open—less buoyant than Alison had been, his movements measured, restrained.

Evening settled in like a velvet cloak, dusted with stars.

The wind eased, leaving only the steady pulse of waves against the rocks. Plates cleared and crumbs brushed away, the girls talked and laughed beneath the pergola, sharing the final stretch of day. James couldn't help but admire the ease in Gabrielle's expression, the way her curls fell back with every burst of joy.

Gabrielle paused, her gaze catching the glow from the string lights before lifting to James. Her smile lingered. "Thank you, again, for this delicious meal."

"My pleasure," James replied, his gaze flickering to Alison—silently urging her to keep the kitchen conversation to herself. She didn't seem inclined to comply.

"Gabrielle showed me a couple of moves earlier—did you see it, Uncle?"

"No," he muttered, eyes dropping to his plate to avoid Alison's gaze.

Her grin widened. "You should've seen her—her dress catching the wind. I swear, she looked like an angel."

"Well, I guess I'll have to see it some other day then," he said, raising his eyebrows at Alison. He gave her a quick nudge with his foot along the firepit's edge. She straightened in her chair, grabbed her plate, and shot him a sly smile.

"Well, I guess it's time for me to go to bed," she replied. "Dad's gonna be mad if I stay up too late..."

Alison walked to the house, leaving them to the fire's warm glow.

"She's quite something," Gabrielle said. "I love her wit."

"Brilliant, but stubborn as hell," James replied. They both laughed.

Gabrielle stood to collect the dishes.

"Oh no—leave it. I'll deal with it tomorrow."

"How about a little dance?"

"What? Dance with you? No way."

"You seemed pretty interested from the kitchen window today."

"Oh—you saw…"

"Pretty hard to miss."

"I'm sorry… I…"

"Don't worry about it," Gabrielle said, brushing it off. "So… wanna dance?"

"I… I don't know how."

"Me neither," she replied, a playful, lopsided grin lighting her lips like a star breaking through the night.

"Very funny."

"Come on. I'll show you." She leaned in, taking his left hand and resting it gently on her waist, while lifting the other into the air. His palms were warm and clammy, betraying his nerves.

"No music?" he asked, raising an eyebrow.

"Music? Nah—I prefer the soundtrack of your nervous heartbeat."

He pressed his lips into a tight line and bit the lower one.

"I haven't been this close to a woman since…"

"I know. It's okay. Let's pretend. Dancing is about letting go of the person we think we are and reaching for what's behind—the Soul. There is no danger here, only peace and grace. This is what my mother taught me," Gabrielle said, moving to the sound of the melody only she could hear.

"Do you like it here?" James asked, carefully following her moves.

"Yes, very much. Why?"

"Oh… nothing. Just that—you seem happier than when you first got here."

With Gabrielle's rhythm guiding him, James let his guard

down. He moved closer, drawn by the warmth and subtle strength of her body, finally allowing himself to surrender.

"Yes. I am. You're very lucky to live here."

You're pretty, he thought, a shy smile moving his lips.

"You're good at this," she continued, her smile warm and encouraging.

"Well, you're a fine dancer yourself," he replied, lifting his hand into the air and swirling her around to end their dance. "Thank you. That was fun."

"It was."

The bright light of the full moon shimmered in their eyes.

"Forgive me for being such an idiot. I didn't mean to spy on you this afternoon—or even lie about it."

"You don't need to apologize. We do strange things when chemistry kicks in."

"Well, I'm glad you like it here," he said, glancing down at his watch. "We need to get up early—time to get some rest."

"You're right. Good night, James," she said, before turning and walking back into the house.

"Good night."

He waited a moment, letting her go inside first. His hands flexed at his sides before he finally stepped toward the house, closing the door behind him and switching off the lights. The kitchen held his footsteps as he made his way upstairs.

On his bed, James lay down, one arm curled behind his head, the scent of burned wood clinging to his hair. How could he be this nervous? Her eyes, her smile, the way she moved—she was like a song he couldn't get out of his head.

The melody hovered above him, and with it came thoughts he hadn't let himself believe in for a long time: Everything in life has its own timing—respecting it has its perks. No need to rush to the finish line when there's no race. Embrace the wait, and let what's meant for you come find you.

He looked out the window at the cloudless sky.

"Yeah," he whispered, "if only it were that simple."

24

UNSPOKEN FAREWELL

The sun rose gently on Gabrielle's last morning at the ranch. It was Alison's last day too—school was looming, and neither wanted summer to end. Alison's begging had earned her a few extra days, but now her time at the ranch was over.

That morning, they sat in the grass, backs against the fence, trying to soak up every last drop—as if they could pack the whole feeling into a doggy bag and take it with them.

"I'm gonna miss this," Alison said. "And I'm gonna miss you."

"I'm going to miss you too," Gabrielle replied, taking in the girl before her. In just a few days, Alison had transformed —her gaze no longer glued to her phone, she took in the world around her with sharp curiosity and vibrant energy. Gabrielle marveled at how fully she'd come into herself in such a short time.

But beneath the spark in her eyes, Gabrielle sensed a remaining concern.

Alison gazed toward the endless horizon and sighed.

Slowly, she edged closer, and with a raw, untamed voice, finally let herself be heard.

"Gabrielle, can I tell you something?"

"Of course. Anything."

"Did you know my mom left? Like I wasn't worth sticking around for... She didn't even say goodbye."

"No, I didn't know. That must've hurt."

Gabrielle's eyes met Alison's. Anger and sadness twisted like a ball of yarn a cat had toyed with for too long.

"She said she wanted nothing to do with us, so she just left. It's been a while now, and we still haven't heard from her. Why would a mother do that?"

Gabrielle paused, then shared the words she knew best— not because she had the answer to Alison's most daunting question, but because it was the right thing to say.

"I know nothing about being a mom, but I can tell you this: her leaving has nothing to do with you. It has everything to do with her. When someone reacts a certain way, it's never because of something you did—their reaction comes from what's going on inside them. You're a wonderful kid; don't forget that. We all have our dark moments. I guess that's just part of being human."

Alison's gaze lingered, hesitant. "I'm afraid she won't ever come back... What about you? What are you most afraid of?"

"Oh—so many things... I don't even know what *doesn't* scare me. Flying, being late, not being loved, even performing. But the worst? Letting go. I hate saying goodbye."

"Like what we're about to do?"

"Yup. I get attached, and then people go. It leaves a hole in my heart. I've gotten better at it, I guess, but I still have a long way to go."

"I don't think there's such a thing as a pleasant goodbye," Alison said.

"Hope there could be. Maybe if we do our best to be grateful for the time we spent together, that might help?"

"Or maybe we could dance instead?"

"That's a great idea. I like that." Gabrielle's smile lifted. She stood and took Alison's hand, guiding her into a gentle spin—letting her know, without words, that she was seen, strong, and enough just as she was. Alison's golden hair fanned out around her, strength sparkling in her eyes. In that moment, Gabrielle understood: random encounters are never random. They are part of something bigger being orchestrated on our behalf.

They danced slowly, sunlight trailing like liquid gold across the grass, until their movements softened and the world seemed to hold its breath. Gabrielle released Alison's hand, and they laughed—joyful and alive. But the sound of a far-off engine reminded them that the fun was coming to an end.

The black BMW rolled up to the ranch. Alison rushed to hug Gabrielle.

"Thank you for everything," she said.

James, standing near the porch, stepped forward and lifted Alison's suitcase into the trunk. Without a word, they said goodbye—their eyes meeting in gratitude and appreciation.

Alison slipped into the car, and James leaned over toward his brother.

"So, how was your trip? Did you get to do what you wanted?"

"And then some…"

"Of course."

"See you soon."

The engine growled as the car pulled away, leaving the

ranch suddenly hollow—like a breath held, waiting for the next one.

Gabrielle stood there, hesitant, meeting James's gaze.

"I should get my things…" she said.

He nodded gently, the unspoken farewell dwelling like the last light at the end of a show, still hopeful for an encore.

As she turned toward the house, her steps faltered. She stopped, then turned back.

"Does it get easier with time?" she asked.

James searched for the right words.

"You mean… grief?"

"Yes."

James exhaled, eyes drifting toward the horizon. He ran a hand behind his head.

"I think it gets easier with trust. Trusting that life will bring the people you need and draw you closer to the ones who need you. One day, you'll find the weight hasn't entirely left—but you'll be stronger under it. And sometimes, it'll even feel like love, not loss."

"That's a nice way of putting it. I'll try to remember that." She shifted her weight, half-turning toward the house, replaying his words in her mind.

"Oh, and Gabrielle… I hope you really get that dream of yours. It's been a pleasure having you here."

"Thank you for making me feel at home." She lowered her head, then stepped inside. When she returned, her hair was neatly tied back, the red ribbon knotted carefully around her ponytail. She placed her suitcase in the car, ready to head into town.

"Take good care of yourself, James…" she said. "Oh, and don't forget the architecture thing."

He smiled back. "I promise."

When she pulled away, her eyes rested in the rearview mirror, tracing the fading silhouette of the house, the land, and him—as if fixing them into memory, a picture she wasn't ready to forget.

But watching it all disappear twisted her heart. This time, she let it sink.

Beneath the ache, she knew the truth: life, in all its complexity, held its own balance—a rhythm of loss and gain, and the promise of something new each time.

THE SOUND OF BREAKING

*A*fter passing by the duty-free perfume shops and restrooms, Gabrielle reached the rolling sidewalks. Even as the city's rhythm hit her the moment she stepped off the plane, she chose not to rush. Instead, she stepped onto the moving carpet and let it carry her forward. Her reflection slid along the glass panels, a smile on her face, a hint of hope caught between who she was and who she was becoming. *You've got this. This year will be different. I promise.*

The crowd from her plane hurried past: parents eager to return home, children still whining after the long ride, a lover dodging faster in anticipation of a long-awaited reunion. Everyone seemed to have a good reason to rush to the other side of the airport walls.

As the moving carpet ended, Gabrielle lifted her suitcase and stepped off. Her smile met the wide-eyed gaze of a child perched high on the father's shoulders. The child paused for a moment before returning her smile.

By the time she reached the exit doors, Gabrielle had

almost convinced herself that the city could be beautiful—that maybe, this time, she could let it in without bracing herself.

She stepped through the revolving glass doors, tucking her luggage close to her feet. A couple pressed in behind her, laughter bubbling between them, their eagerness pushing the doors faster until she had no choice but to hurry through.

Outside, the heat washed over her like an unexpected wave —the traffic wild and feral, horns and sirens snarling from every direction. She tightened her grip on the suitcase handle and steered toward the taxi lane. Nadia didn't know she had returned; Gabrielle wanted it to be a surprise. Her chest rose with anticipation. She had somewhere to go, and a dream to chase.

But the crowd surged around her, elbows and backpacks jostling. The sun baked her shoulders; sweat dripped into her hair, and cabs were nowhere to be found, the lane blocked by an accident. Taken aback, she slid into the nearest rest area, pressed her back against the grimy window, and let herself catch a moment of calm, searching for the inner peace that had come so easily by the sea.

She dug into her bag to get her phone. It vibrated faintly in her palm as she switched off airplane mode. A red voicemail notification blinked on her screen. She tapped it and brought the phone to her ear.

"Hi Gabrielle, it's Rachel. I'm calling about your enrollment. Unfortunately, we won't be able to take you on this year. You didn't send your payment, and frankly, we weren't comfortable with you coming back so soon after... everything. I'm sorry. You can take some time and reapply next year. Stop by the school when you're in town. We'll have your things—"

The phone slipped from her hands, clattering against the

pavement, the glass cracking like brittle ice. The sound rang louder than it should have—like fate striking a verdict.

An old man walking by paused, bent down, and picked it up. He handed it back with a slight bow, his spine stooped with age.

"Here... you dropped this," he said.

Gabrielle gave a shaky nod. "Thanks... I—yeah, thanks."

The man eased upright and shuffled back into the crowd. She sank to the sidewalk, her suitcase her only support. Rachel's words didn't settle—they mutated in her mind, sharpening into a life sentence: it was over. *All of it.*

Her breath caught. Her hands shook. She tried to push herself up, but her legs—hollow, incapable—refused to hold her.

She sank back down.

The music. The dance. The studio that had held her in her most vulnerable moments—snatched away, and her heart, heavy and weightless at once, fell through the cracks of her own life. Much like her reflection in the broken glass, her thoughts fractured—splintered shards, each dangerous on their own. The buzz of the city hovered at the edges of her mind: voices, horns, the shriek of a bus's brakes. It all pressed against her awareness, sharp and unyielding, mocking her fate.

The future she had been building since her mother's passing dismantled before her eyes, leaving only blank space where life used to be. It was like losing her a second time.

Memories surged over her like a life review. The clean scent of the studio the first morning they came in. The sound of her shoes striking the freshly coated wood. The taste of sweat and adrenaline in her mouth. That world no longer belonged to her—more like a borrowed identity, suddenly reclaimed by its owner. Unreal, as if it had never existed.

Travelers rushed for their bus, hustling past her. One of them struck Gabrielle's suitcase, sending it skidding across the ground, her clothes spilling out in a heap.

A scream burst from her gut, raw and wrenching, tearing itself free before she could stop it. It was not the cry of a girl but the howl of an animal being cornered, stripped of everything. Heads turned, and for one breath, the entire sidewalk stood still, transfixed by the rupture of sound.

Then the city moved on. Feet hurried. Bags rolled. A woman muttered something about "lunatics."

Gabrielle bent forward, clutching her stomach, the scream still echoing in her chest. This time, tears didn't come. Instead, something fiercer and darker stirred inside her, like embers flaring in a still-burning pit. Her voice cracked, rattling the words as her lips trembled, jaw tight.

"Please... not again."

She sank to the ground, knees giving out, the sting of heat burning across her skin.

26
NIGHT MOVES

*T*hat night, Gabrielle had a hard time falling asleep. She had told Nadia everything—about her father's carpenter, Rachel's call, even the notebook her mother had left behind—but sharing it all only made the weight heavier. As she tossed and turned, millions of stars shone with a light so bright she wondered if the universe had something to tell her.

Lying on her back, she stared at the emptiness of the ceiling, the light of the moon reflecting on it. Could it all be connected? What if there had been signs, and she just hadn't seen them? Her mind couldn't let go—if there was a meaning to all this, she needed to find it.

The book.

Gabrielle rose and opened the wardrobe. She reached for her suitcase, pulled out her mother's notebook, and climbed back onto her bed. Bathed in the crisp blue halo of full moonlight, she opened it carefully. The pages were still blank —but this time, something caught her eye: a loose sheet at the back, slipping slightly from its binding. She eased it free and let her eyes fall upon the words:

Dear Soul,

May our words bring you comfort in a time when struggles seem to shadow your every thought.

We are the Land Keepers—souls living in a world next to yours, just at the edge of sleep and awareness. Like golden owls in the night, we watch over you as you walk the path to your destiny, making sure you never lose sight of the light in your heart.

First, understand this: there is no right or wrong path—only the one that speaks most deeply to you.

But how do you know whether you are walking within the boundaries of your own journey, or trespassing into the realms of another? It isn't always easy—but it is simple.

Follow the light in your heart.

Every human is born with a purpose. Most will never find it, for they cannot see the signs, let alone follow them. The rare few who do are what we call Soul Travelers. They can never know true fulfilment until they dwell fully in the light of their heart.

You are one of them.

And know this: for every struggle, there is a secret gateway to what you are seeking. Follow the *signs—they will lead you to the reason you came here.*

Lovingly,
The Land Keepers

As she finished reading, memories poured down like a river held by a single thread. The light from the place she had come from, her mother's words, her longing for dance, Miles's touch, James's smile as he handed her the notebook—they all surfaced at once, forming patterns she hadn't noticed before, like puzzle pieces of a hidden tapestry.

She knew what she had to do.

Without hesitation, she left the apartment and made her way to school. The moon glowed overhead, casting silver light across the empty streets. At the school entrance, she swiped her card, and the doors opened with a soft click. She stepped into the elevator, pressed the button for the sixth floor, and felt the gentle hum as it rose through the stillness of the night.

She spotted the concierge wiping the floors near the studio. She walked toward him, each step echoing in the empty hall.

"Oh—hi, Miss Gabrielle… What are you doing here at this hour?"

"I couldn't sleep and thought I'd review my choreography before our class," she said. "Would you mind letting me in for a few hours?"

He chuckled and adjusted his glasses. "Ah, the full moon, huh? Keeps me up too. But technically, I'm not supposed to let anyone in."

"I just need this one session," she said, her voice steady, filled with firm resolve.

"You've always struck me as disciplined and hardworking. Fine—go on. But be out before eight—or I'll have to tell the boss I let you sneak in." His lips stretched awkwardly across his cheeks, showing his misaligned teeth. He walked to the studio door, leaning on one leg as he dug into his pocket for a ring of keys. After unlocking the door, he held it open for Gabrielle, nodding for her to enter.

"Thank you. I'll be out before you even notice," she said.

Gabrielle stepped into the lobby, opened the door to Studio 1, and left the lights low. She slid on her headphones and danced to the rhythm of every song she knew—rock 'n' roll, country, pop, jazz. For hours, her body moved to the music, each note unlocking pieces of herself she had long forgotten. Her wounds—half-healed, half-redeemed—pierced through her soaked clothes.

When the last note faded, Gabrielle stood tall. In front of the floor-to-ceiling mirrors, she met her wide, green eyes, wet ginger curls clinging to her face, and smiled. "I've got this."

Morning was approaching, but before she could gather herself and leave, the door opened. The receptionist had come in early.

"It's good to see you back, Gabrielle."

"Oh! You scared me."

"How did you get in?"

"I... asked the concierge for a favor. I needed one last session before—"

"They're kicking you out, right?"

"So you've heard?"

"Such a shame. But don't worry—I won't tell a soul."

"Thank you. I'll leave before anyone else sees me." Gabrielle grabbed her bag and moved toward the door.

"I'd hate myself if I didn't tell you this…"

"Tell me what?"

"A New York agent is coming in this morning. He's picking someone for an upcoming play. I think you deserve a shot."

"But that could ruin my chances of reapplying next year."

"Maybe… but after what I just saw? I think you have a real chance. Auditions start at nine. Think about it."

"I hope it won't get you into trouble," Gabrielle said.

"Let's just say a friend of yours gave you a heads-up."

"Thanks."

"Now… you should go."

Gabrielle stepped out into the morning air, the streets slowly stirring to life. Delivery trucks rumbled past, joggers traced the sidewalks, and office workers hurried along, coffee in hand. She moved among them like a ghost, wet hair sticking to the side of her face, clothes glued to her skin. Her stomach rumbled. She dug into her bag and pulled out a protein bar, took a distracted bite, then stopped halfway. Nausea churned. She folded the wrapper and shoved it back into her bag.

She circled the block, careful to avoid the other students heading in. When she spotted Nadia, she waved her over from behind the brick wall.

"What are you doing, hiding here?" Nadia asked, eyes wide.

"Listen—I don't have time to explain. There's a secret audition this morning, and I want to sneak in."

Nadia frowned. "Oh, no… that doesn't sound like a good plan."

"I'm willing to risk it. Let's be honest—would you come back, after knowing what they did?"

"Nope."

"Me neither. So, I'm going to walk in and take my chance."

Nadia exhaled, then nodded. "Okay. What can I do to help?"

"Text me when the last person goes in."

"Got it."

An hour later, the receptionist stepped to the audition-room doorway. "Any more contestants?" she called, her voice carrying across the hall.

Gabrielle raised a hand before she could talk herself out of it. "Yes," she said. "Me."

She stepped past the receptionist and into the audition room. The space buzzed with chatter and nerves. Nadia brushed her hand as she passed. "You've got this," she whispered.

The moment Gabrielle crossed the threshold, a hush rippled through the room. Heads turned. Rachel's lips pressed into a thin, disbelieving line.

"You can't—" Rachel pushed to her feet, agitation flaring.

Beside her, the NY agent stood just as fast, catching her arm. "Sit," he said. "I want to see her."

Gabrielle froze, every nerve sparking as she moved toward the center of the room. The stage lights poured over her, too bright, too revealing. Her breathing stuttered; her palms slicked with nerves. Still, she stepped forward—one careful foot, then another.

The door swung shut behind her with a final click.

27

WHEN THE MUSIC STARTS

G abrielle stood still in the middle of the stage, her eyes fixed on an invisible target. Her feet glued to the floor, she lifted her chin a few inches, took a deep breath and closed her eyes. Soft violins began to play in the background, their notes filling the air with the scent of rose petals and the taste of the past. It was the song her mother danced to each morning.

Upon hearing the first notes, Gabrielle would wake up, climb out of her bed and tiptoe down the stairs. Eyes peeking through the rail into the living room, her tiny hands clutching the posts in awe, watching her mother move gracefully, as if in conversation with the Goddess of music herself.

Rachel, bent over her notes, wrapped up a comment on the previous contestant before looking back up, her jaw set tight. Beside her, the stranger from New York adjusted his dark-framed glasses, curiosity creasing his brow as he leaned forward slightly. With his aubergine suit and sleek shoes—he looked every bit the part of someone who wasn't there by accident.

But Gabrielle didn't notice. Her chest thrummed with energy, her sorrows dissolving with every movement her body made. With remarkable ease, her spirit fully embodied the raw pulse of life itself—a pure relationship with bliss. Lost in the glow of her mother's spirit, she rose above the tension that filled the room.

After the last note, Gabrielle left the stage, stepping into the lobby as if surfacing from deep water. Murmurs of students drifted around her—jealous girls huddled in a corner, trading side-eyed glances and tucking whispers behind cupped hands.

At the desk, the receptionist leaned back, hands folded neatly, a pleased expression settling on her face as she watched Gabrielle.

Nadia shifted from foot to foot, fingers nervously tapping on the bench. When Gabrielle walked toward her, she rushed forward and wrapped her in a full embrace.

With the auditions over, everyone gathered by the familiar row of lockers, waiting for the final verdict.

The studio door creaked, and Rachel appeared, peeking through the opening.

"We have a slight situation to address, but I'll get back to you with the results very soon." Her eyes swept the lobby until they met Gabrielle's. She pointed. "You. Come with me."

Rachel's jaw tightened as Gabrielle approached. She closed the door after her and leaned in, "You weren't supposed to be here today. You know that."

"You said my courses were over. You never said I couldn't audition," Gabrielle said, meeting Rachel's gaze without flinching.

The agent stood and stepped between them, eyebrows raised. "Wait—what's going on here?"

Rachel's face flushed. "I... had to make some hard decisions this year. Gabrielle wasn't supposed to be here."

"But I just watched her dance," he said, his voice intensifying. "That was extraordinary." He turned to Gabrielle. "Explain."

Gabrielle felt her cheeks burn. "My father passed away this summer, and I... I wasn't able to send my payment on time. Rachel thought I should take a pause from the program and try again next year."

His expression hardened as he looked at Rachel.

"You kicked her out over a late payment?"

"It's not just that," Rachel said defensively. "She's been through a lot. I thought it would be better for her—"

"Better for her—or for you?" His voice sliced through her excuse like a knife through churned butter. He turned back to Gabrielle. "I came here looking for the strongest performer. What I saw in you today is exactly what we need."

Rachel stepped back. "Max, I don't think she's ready for something like that—"

"With respect, Rachel, that's not your call anymore." His square face and sharp jawline seemed carved from precious stones. His light brown eyes, perfectly symmetrical, set above a neatly trimmed beard. He sat back on his chair and invited Gabrielle to sit next to him.

He leaned in and dropped his elbows onto his thighs. "Gabrielle, let me be honest. I can't imagine what it's like to lose someone you deeply care about, but the way you showed up today—putting your heart on the floor for us to feel— shows how profoundly capable you are. Your performance was a true gift: technically demanding, yet utterly original." He glanced at Rachel, fidgeting with her clipboard. "Sometimes the best artists come from the most unexpected places."

He stood, hands sliding into the pockets of his wrinkle-free trousers. "I want to offer you a chance to come to New York. You'd study alongside professional dancers and assist with the show's repetitions. It's not exactly a job, nor a typical school program. But from what I understand, you won't really have another shot here next year. So... what do you think?"

"But... I'm far from good enough to work with professionals," Gabrielle said, holding back, afraid to dive into the excitement too soon. She stood still, feet together, arms folded across her chest.

"Maybe not today, I agree. But let me be clear, Gabrielle—sometimes schools have a way of dulling great potential." He shot a pointed look at Rachel. "No offense, but that's the reality of formal education." He glanced back at Gabrielle. "What I'm offering is different—more like an internship where you'd learn as you go. We need someone like you: young, passionate, a soul with an edge. And Gabrielle, you have that." His voice was deep, hypnotizing.

Rachel cleared her throat. "Max, perhaps we should discuss—"

"There's nothing to discuss—I've made my choice," Max said. He turned back to Gabrielle. "Now it's up to you... Are you in?"

Gabrielle sat there for a moment, letting it all sink in. The drop of adrenaline, mixed with a sleepless night, had taken its toll. Her chest throbbed with the pulse of possibility, and a fire well-lit sparked behind her eyes. She exhaled, letting the tension slide from her shoulders and out of her chest.

"Yes," she said, her voice steady. "I'm in."

Max's lips curved into a smile. Rachel's mouth opened, as if to protest, but no words came out.

Gabrielle felt a thrill ripple through her, the kind that comes when the world shifts, just slightly, but enough to tilt everything forward. And for the first time in a long while, the future felt like a place she might actually want to be.

28
TAKING FLIGHT

*I*n Gabrielle's world, dancing was not only an art—it was a tribute. Each step was a way to hold her mother close, honor her spirit, and keep alive a bond that loss had threatened to sever. That devotion shaped her identity, carried her through girlhood, and lit the path to this very moment.

Yet, standing at the front stage of her new life—boarding pass to New York clutched in her hand—something inside her shifted. Perhaps there was no single "right" path. Perhaps every road, if walked with heart, could lead her back home.

That belief carried her forward as she stood in line at the airport luggage counter two weeks after the unexpected turn of events, her suitcase packed with both new dreams and new dance clothes. Even amid the turmoil of another farewell, she couldn't help but smile at her friend's irrepressible enthusiasm. Nadia wouldn't have missed this celebration for anything.

"Oh, my goodness! This is so exciting," Nadia said. "I can't believe you actually got the part! New York, here she comes!"

"Calm down, Nad—you'll alert security."

"They'll never stop me!" Nadia said as she tossed her thick black hair out of her face, her energy practically lifting the roof. "Can you believe this? You're going to be a star! Just promise me you won't pull any of the crazy stunts I would."

"A star? Don't you think you're exaggerating a little?" Gabrielle said, pulling out her passport.

Behind the rope, Nadia practically spun in place, excitement crackling off her. "Exaggerating? Girl, are you blind or what? When will you ever start believing in yourself? You're a star—a real one."

Gabrielle gave a soft shrug as she hefted her suitcase onto the scale. "I don't know. I just want to do what I love; that's all."

The woman behind the counter gave her a nod. "It's light enough—you can bring it on the plane."

"Thank you," Gabrielle said, grabbing her luggage and edging away from the crowd.

She glanced back at Nadia just in time to see her fling her arms wide, as if ready to hug the entire line of passengers.

"Come on, don't leave me hanging! I'm going to miss you, sunshine."

"I'll miss you too," Gabrielle replied, softening into her embrace.

Nadia released the hug and smoothed back Gabrielle's curls, which had spiraled tighter in the humid air, and pressed close.

"Let me know how it goes, okay?"

"I will," Gabrielle said slowly, loosening her grip.

They each wiped a tear from their eyes, and Gabrielle carried her heart through one more goodbye. As she stepped to the front of the line, she handed over her passport, passed through security, and emerged on the other side. Turning the last visible corner, she waved to her friend one last time.

She walked through the terminal, the bustle of travelers and the hum of departures fading around her as she carried her thoughts forward. Passing cafés and small shops, she let her gaze wander until she reached the bookstore. Dropping her backpack to the floor, she unzipped the front pocket and tucked her passport safely inside. She pulled her sweater from the bag and slipped it on, savoring the soft weight against her skin.

As she slid her phone into the front pocket, Gabrielle felt the vibration of a new message. *Nad already?* she wondered—before realizing the text wasn't from her.

It was from James.

Her heartbeat took off, tightening the knot of anxiety in her chest.

> "Hey Gabrielle! Hope all's good with you. Just wanted to say hi. Decided to give the architecture thing a shot again. Rusty like an old wagon, but I guess that means I've held my promise."

Gabrielle's face lit up. She glanced around, as if hoping to share her excitement with someone, then looked back down at her phone and typed:

> "That's amazing! So proud of you. Things are starting to look up over here too—I got offered an internship in NY. Can hardly believe it. About to hop on the plane."

James replied almost instantly, his surprise spilling through the text:

"What?! That's unbelievable. Well... I mean,
you totally deserve it..."

"I know... I figured someone had to keep you
on your toes."

"Ha! Very funny..."

Just then, the announcement cut in: "Priority passengers on the flight to New York are asked to proceed to gate one for boarding. I repeat, priority passengers may now proceed to gate one."

Gabrielle glanced at her ticket. PRIORITY. She grinned and typed one last message:

"Gotta go. But we'll keep in touch, right?"

"Absolutely. Can't wait. Have a safe flight."

As she stepped onto the plane and found her seat, Gabrielle pulled out her mother's notebook and flipped it open. A folded piece of paper fell out, tucked between the white pages. Her eyes widened, like a child on Christmas morning. Carefully, she unfolded it.

Around her, passengers stowed bags and settled in, but Gabrielle couldn't contain her curiosity. She began to read.

To my beautiful pumpkin,
The doctors were clear. If all went well, I
could expect to live for a few months. It has
been a year. My secret? You. I just couldn't

bear the idea of leaving you to this world without me by your side—smiling at all your little quirks. I would've given everything for just one last breath in your fiery curls, one last hug goodnight, one last glance at you sleeping tight.

Gabrielle, you are my proudest moment, my daily gratitude, the strip of life I cannot let go of.

In the end, your father helped me walk to your room. I stood there, watching you, for as long as my legs could hold me.

Tonight, the stars shine brighter than usual; they know something I will soon find out.

But there is one thing I have to tell you before I leave. I have glimpsed the beauty of a world next to ours—they call it the Unseen. There are multiple doorways to reach this place, but delicate balance is required. We must respect it and tread lightly.

For myself, I've traveled there through my dreams, always returning with even greater eagerness to share what I had discovered. Your father knew, though he had a hard time imagining it, so I did my best to honor his understanding. I have written everything I know inside these pages. May it find you delighted and blessed.

I do not want to leave this body, yet something is calling me—something that will allow me to do the work I couldn't accomplish here. The work that will guide another, and perhaps, in time, uncover parts of my own past—parts that might, one day, help you understand who you are.

The light shines brighter now. I hope it won't wake you.

Your father has fallen asleep in the chair next to my bed. It makes me wonder: have I truly savored all that life had to offer? Most definitely not. Have I sown seeds that will one day grow into marvelous trees, offering their shade for others to enjoy? I like to think so.

May you find the courage to pursue your dreams, build a family of your own, and change the trajectory of life itself. These are the real treasures I have seen.

Love,
Charlotte

The pilot spoke his instructions for takeoff.

Gabrielle closed her mother's notebook and tucked it into the pocket of the seat in front of her. She sat up straight, head held high. She buckled in, half-relieved, half-excited. The change she had been waiting for had finally arrived—not without scars, but with a full heart ready to embrace the light of a brand-new day.

As the wheels rolled and the engines roared, Gabrielle couldn't stop thinking about all the things her mother had longed to share. Securely stored within the pages of a book, the answers to life's questions lay in wait.

And, as faithful as a dog anticipating its master, the Unseen lingered patiently—ready to unravel its mysteries and flood her with the truths her soul had been longing for.

ENJOYED *TREASURES OF THE UNSEEN*?

If the story spoke to you, I'd be grateful if you left a review. Your words help other readers discover the book—and keep its message reaching new hearts. Thank you!

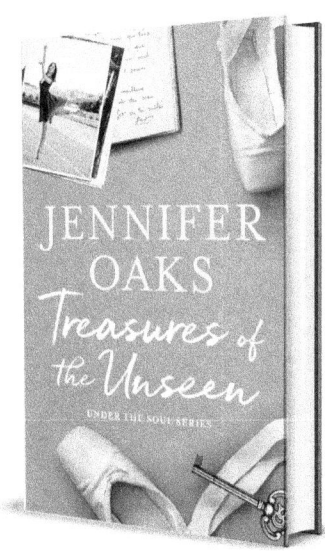

DON'T WANT TO MISS A THING?

Head over to **jenniferoaks.kit.com/newsletter** and join Jennifer's newsletter. Inside, you'll find subtle hints and guiding clues to help you trace the secret thread running through the series—along with a personal tracker to keep track of the hidden clues you uncover.

WANT MORE?

The **Under the Soul Series** continues…

In **BEHIND THE SEEN**, a new world opens before Gabrielle—one filled with wonders that make destiny feel undeniably real. As her relationships deepen and her love for who she is grows, extraordinary things begin to unfold. Each moment sends ripples through the lives of those she meets, reminding us that every encounter matters and every moment is part of a greater design.

Turn the page to begin Book 2.

BEHIND THE SEEN (BOOK 2)

PROLOGUE

The chase seemed endless.

Gabrielle stopped to catch her breath. She looked around—thick trees surrounded her, muddy pathways meandering toward unknown places. The air was cold, heavy with the damp smell of mold. Nothing reassuring. Nowhere to hide.

The shed was too far away to even consider going back. She wouldn't have enough time to escape. And besides, they would discover the treasure it sheltered. Gabrielle couldn't let that happen either—so she kept running.

The air racing through her lungs burned like wild flames eager to consume the last molecules of oxygen, stealing what little strength she had left. Exhausted and out of breath, she collapsed to the ground.

The earth beneath was cold and slick, as if it had been raining for days. The wind was sharp and unforgiving, carrying the promise of snow—a whole lot of it. The sun, unable to pierce through the forest's thick canopy, had already abandoned its warming task and was quickly sinking below the horizon.

Gabrielle knew she had to keep moving.

In an attempt to pull herself up, she reached for a branch above her head. As she stood, it cracked—a sharp sound echoed deep into the forest. The fall was even harder this time.

"How can I get out of this?" she whispered, the adrenaline slowly wearing off. Her legs—bruised and aching—could no longer support her. She stayed pressed against the moss.

Behind her, a man's voice drew close. Too close.

"She's here somewhere," he said. "I know it…"

For the first time, Gabrielle felt she was staring death in the face—and for a moment, the weight of her own life pressed against her ribs: the passing of her mother, the roots she never got to keep, the love she let slip through her fingers.

"Come on… wake up. You have to wake up."

Usually, when bad dreams occurred, Gabrielle knew she could control them. With a simple, practiced intention, she could escape the terror of those too-frequent nightmares and find herself back in her bed.

But this time, the attempt didn't work.

Her heart tightened. "I don't want to die," she pleaded. "Not until I've truly loved."

She exhaled a deep breath and closed her eyes. Her mother's words rippled back into view, like rocks skipping across a silvered pond:

"Cross the bridge and find the sacred shed. It will be a small, blackened timber hut, windowless, with one door. Step inside, and you will see many treasures—but only one is meant for you. It rests within a singing bowl, perched upon the highest shelf. Take it. Whatever comes, it will keep you safe."

Before the chase began, Gabrielle had found the shed. It

was exactly as her mother had described: windowless, with a single door. Inside, the air bore a peculiar darkness, cradling the seed of a new tomorrow—the scent of life reborn, a fresh existence rising from the ashes—the seed of growth, as she would call it.

"I have the treasure, Mother; now what?"

But before a response could reach her, something in the woods caught her off guard. She strained to see through the tangle of trunks and underbrush, her heart hammering.

A branch snapped in front of her.

"Grab my hand," a warm voice intoned.

She blinked through the shadow, and two perfectly round eyes stared back at her, slowly coming into focus.

"Who are you?" she asked.

A hand yanked her from the mud and into the warmth of a large fur cape. She gasped at the surprising strength of the pull as he hoisted her onto his back, as if she weighed no more than a handful of feathers.

"Hold on tight," he said.

Like the force of the tide, the man ran, sure-footed and relentless, as if the forest itself had already whispered its secrets to him.

Soon the trail narrowed. Hundred-year-old trees and massive moss-draped rocks blocked the way.

The treasure in hand, Gabrielle threw one of the stones she had found in the shed, as if she knew its purpose. The moment it struck the ground, flames leapt among the ancient trunks.

"Don't stop," she urged, instinct guiding her words.

After some time, the man finally stopped and helped her to her feet. Behind them, fire licked the bark of the old trees.

"I think you're out of danger for now," he said. "The

coming snow should take care of the fire." His gaze dropped to the bruises on her leg. "I have what you need to heal that. Come with me."

They stepped to the edge of the land, and a serene valley unfolded before them. In the distance, a small cabin waited, smoke curling from the chimney. Its walls, built from reclaimed wood, glowed in the fading light. The front door, hand-painted a gentle yellow, seemed to promise a warm hug.

"This is my place," he continued.

Gabrielle hesitated for a moment, then let herself follow, her legs still shaky, her mind spinning with everything that had just happened. "It... looks like heaven," she said, the words tasting unfamiliar in her mouth.

"It is," he replied, leading her inside. "Let me prepare something warm for you to drink, and I'll take a look at those bruises."

She sank into the couch, letting the cabin's warmth press against her skin. Her eyes closed for just a moment—just long enough to feel the fire seep into her bones.

By the time he returned with the tea, Gabrielle had drifted into sleep, her body fully surrendering to rest.

He set the cup on the table beside her, then gently rolled up the legs of her pants and cleaned the wounds with fresh water and medicinal herbs.

When it was done, he draped a blanket over her, tucking it snugly around her as if shielding her from the world. He stood and paused, studying the woman he had saved. Questions swirled through his mind like a tropical storm—why was she here and why was she being hunted.

As he turned, a small, restless shift in her sleep sent something tumbling to the floor. He bent to scoop up the rough pieces, their dark edges catching the moonlight—strange and out of place.

"Lava stones? Where did you get those?"

He glanced back at her, still asleep.

Turning each thoughtfully, he slipped them into his own pocket. "I guess that will have to wait until morning."

Then, a green glow suddenly appeared around her, a brilliant swirl of ancient jade and pure white, dancing like fairies above a fire pit. One by one, he switched off the cabin lights, leaving a single lamp dimmed—just enough to capture Gabrielle's halo.

"This woman is here for you," he heard a voice say. "She holds the key to what you've been searching for."

He knew the voice well—wise beyond years. Some might call it intuition; he knew better than to think that—but following its advice had never been his strong suit.

He shook his head and walked to his room.

Stacks of old journals filled the closet, left there long before his arrival on the land. Each page recorded strange occurrences, careful observations, insights from those who had been here before. Wisdom beyond his own often revealed itself in their words, deepening his curiosity about the voice he was hearing.

He pulled a journal from the pile. Flipping through the pages, his fingers stopped on a fated passage—one that seemed meant for him.

You are energy... very pure in your being. When you come near another, your energy touches the space—and those inside. The aura shows the gifts you bring to share. The gifts? They show in the colors you make. When others see your hues, it means they are in the same rhythm as you, and can help your gifts grow. Remember, you are not separate. What you see... it is of you. What you are... it is of that.

He glanced in the mirror next to his bed. He could see Gabrielle sleeping in the reflection, her face lit by the moon, soft on her cheeks. He lowered his head and continued reading.

All lights... they are good. They show many ways to know life. All light teaches. In body, in mind... in soul.

"How is that even supposed to help?" he said, closing the journal on his lap.

A sudden chill swept through the cabin. His eyes darted to the couch—she was gone. Only the green and white of her halo lingered for a moment, still dancing in the dim light.

To be continued...

JOIN THE WAITLIST
The
UNDER THE SOUL
MAIL CLUB
When everything drifts away—find peace and start anew.
UNDER THE SOUL
COMING THIS SUMMER
WWW.JENNIFEROAKS.COM/LETTERS

ABOUT THE AUTHOR

JENNIFER OAKS writes fiction that blends modern life with the heart's longing for meaning. Her work is carefully layered with mystical vibes and hidden clues, inviting readers to trust what they feel as much as what they see.

She was eight years old when she heard her dream for the first time. Sitting at her desk, she wrote *"Love Stories"* at the top of a blank page. The dream pulsed again in high school when she won second place in a writing contest—a red ribbon she would later weave into *Treasures of the Unseen* as a deeper clue to meaning. But it was reading *The Alchemist* that turned it all into a calling many years later. Since then, writing has become a true passion.

Jennifer moved 33 times in 46 years before settling into her cottage in Eastern Canada, where she lives as a mother of two and an advocate for simple living. She also loves turning her funny little drawings into stickers—and spending long moments staring at the trees.

www.jenniferoaks.com

instagram.com/novelsbyjenniferoaks
facebook.com/novelsbyjenniferoaks
pinterest.com/novelsbyjenniferoaks

ACKNOWLEDGMENTS

Writing takes dedication and courage. When you're looking back at what you have accomplished, all those long hours, late nights and early mornings spent on your computer putting words one after the other; you know you have sacrificed a piece of your own life to share your passion with the world. Taking a moment to be grateful for those who made it possible, becomes a must.

For that, I want to thank my lover and my two boys for their patience and support while writing this book. This story took over ten years to write, and I couldn't have done it without them. Thank you to my family for believing in me when writing a book was just a dream. You have been the fertile soil from which I could bloom.

A special thanks to my fantastic team: Sarah & Liam. You have made this book possible. Not only with better words, or beautiful pictures but with the vibe and spirit I wanted this story to convey. Your hard work made my dream a reality.

I also want to thank you, the reader. Strangely enough, I've always thought I would write for myself. I tried to create what I couldn't find but wanted to read. But while writing this book, I discovered that I was not only writing for myself but I was mostly writing for you.

I write for that part of you that is scared to love — that part of you wondering if Life sometimes offers a break when you can be happy and fulfilled. I write for the part of you that does not trust, the part that has been hurt or forgotten. I write for the inner child you had to leave behind to become an adult. I write wishing he would come back.

May you find, in the words I have put before you, a quiet place to come to and a confirmation that you are not alone. That Life, as well as people who love you, are there for you. I am grateful for the door you left open so that this book could find you. I am thankful to you. Thank you.